A Mean Piece

of Water

By

Jes McCutchen

MANUSTRIUM
MEDIA

Manustrium Media
848 S Indianapolis Ave
Tulsa OK 74112

Cover Illustration | Ezra Blank
Cover Design | Maxi Vittor
Editor | Jeni Chappelle
Editor | Racheal Daodu

Library of Congress Control Number | 2022917238

ISBN | 979-8-9859486-2-2 (eBook)
ISBN | 979-8-9859486-3-9 (Paperback)

Also, by Jes McCutchen

Chronicles of My Alien Invasion Life

Content Warnings:

Please take care of yourself, and reach out to me on social media if you have any questions or would like more details about the CWs.

Blood
Animal attacks
Taxidermy
Body Horror
Cults
Anxiety

If you or someone you know is possibly in a cult PLEASE don't take anything in the book as advice. It is not.

988 is the US national mental health crisis and suicide prevention hotline. Take care of you and yours, friends.

"You're in a cult. Call your dad."

This one is for M.R.H.

Chapter 1 Kye

Kye took the flyer from the Church of the Flood and tucked it in their back pocket as they left the gas station with supplies for dinner. There weren't many other places in town for groceries or for members to hand out pamphlets explaining their bonkers theories, so everyone in town was used to passing by them into and out of the convenience store.

They would usually just toss the flyer in the trash can, but it felt awkward with the four members staring right at them, including one who looked like she could have been at school with Kye, so Kye just mumbled "thanks" and took off, hot dogs and marshmallows tucked safely in the basket on their bicycle. Their parents had fully stocked the fridge with enough food for a month, but Kye wanted s'mores.

Florence would be at Lake Hobotnica this afternoon, and the two of them actually had the house to themselves for all of spring break. It was going to be glorious.

Kye was really grateful when their parents let them stay at home for the week, when their mom had gotten called to a work trip last minute. Usually, Kye would have had to tag along, but they pointed out that soon they'd be on their own anyway so why not start a couple months early?

It had taken some convincing, but Florence's parents were on board as well, which was extremely exciting.

Florence's therapist had actually recommended it since her panic attacks were more frequent as she got closer to graduation. She hadn't said as much outright, but Kye knew her anxiety was getting worse and time at the lake always made her feel better.

Most of this break's plans comprised of watching movies and napping.

There was no cell phone reception at the lake, and the internet was slow as could be and not usually even worth trying to use. So Kye and Florence wouldn't even have to think about social media, and the prospect was blissful. Just board games and reading and Molly Ringwald DVD collection marathons and piles of s'mores with their best friend for a whole week.

They were daydreaming about what that might look like and taking their time on the hilly road where the pavement was smooth, when halfway home, Bruno trotted out of the woods and started loping along beside their bike. Kye stopped for a second, reaching over to scratch the tall dog behind the ears. He was tall enough they didn't have to bend to reach his big head. He lazily wagged his tail, and Kye noticed with annoyance that Bruno was muddy up to his belly and would need rinsed off before he could go inside.

Kye also noticed something alive in his mouth.

"Bruno, what in the world are you tryin' to eat?" They put on the kickstand and stepped off their bike. Pointing at the ground, they commanded, "Drop it."

Bruno gave Kye a withering look that was simultaneously bored and annoyed. But he obediently dropped the giant bullfrog onto the ground.

"You're such a gross dog. What the heck are you doing with Emmylou?" Kye laughed. The large American bullfrog was unharmed, which was good news because Dani would be beside herself if anything happened to her pet.

Emmylou just let out a loud croak.

Kye scooped up Emmylou and placed her—they were pretty sure she was a her anyway, sort of hard to tell with a frog—into the basket on the front of their bike, on top of the bag of hot dog buns.

"You two been off on a little animal adventure?" Kye got back onto their bike after giving Bruno another scratch. "Come on, we gotta get her into some water before Dani finds out and never throws another stick for you to fetch."

3

The rest of the bike ride back to their lake home was peaceful. They took the longer route that gave the best views.

Hopefully, this week would help settle Florence so she could make it through the rest of the school year. Kye was so ready to graduate high school. Then in the fall, Kye and Florence would be at the same school for the first time, which they'd dreamed about for years. Their plan was to room together in a small apartment and get their prerequisite classes done at the community college in Tulsa.

It was far enough away to feel independent, not so far they couldn't visit Lake Hobotnica and their parents on the weekends when they wanted to. Or when they had laundry to do.

It was their tiny school they were most ready to say good riddance to. Maybe they would do a fireworks celebration when it was closer to graduation or even some sort of pyre where they could burn anything with the school mascot on it.

Thinking of summer, Kye couldn't help but daydream about the first hot day when diving into the lake would give that perfect whole-body relief. They'd be swimming in the lake way before then, but there was nothing like breaking through the sweltering Oklahoma heat with a cool dip.

Today, it was rather cloudy for springtime, and the water seemed a bit disturbed. It was far too cold for them to be swimming anyway, so it really didn't matter.

But Dani had promised to come by, and that made Kye's stomach do a flip-floppy thing. It wouldn't surprise them if Dani was already on her way over. Given the fact that Emmylou Harris had turned up with Bruno, she'd be on the search.

Florence had written a short story that she wanted to read to them, and Dani and Kye decided to make it a celebration since, even just a summer ago, Florence was so shy about her writing that she would never have volunteered to read some of it aloud. Kye wasn't totally sure what they wanted to study after high school, but Florence had been thinking about being an author for her whole life.

Kye passed across the property line and felt the familiar sense of protection as they biked the rest of the way down their gravel drive.

Leaning the bike on the side of the house, they carefully extracted Emmylou and put her in a tub of water on the back deck before beckoning Bruno over so they could rinse off his dirt-caked paws. Emmylou made it more difficult by hopping over to sit directly under his belly the whole time.

If Kye had to guess, the two were conspiring to ensure they couldn't use shampoo since it wouldn't be good for Bruno's bullfrog friend and he hated it.

After that chore was done, Kye put away the groceries and grabbed a couple of treats for the pets, a rawhide for Bruno and a few dead June bugs they scooped up for Emmylou, who slurped them up with happy crunches.

A glance at the clock told them they had a few hours before Florence was scheduled to arrive, so popping in headphones, they settled into the hammock for a nap. Bruno walked over and plopped Emmylou into Kye's lap just as they got comfortable.

"Eww, but fine."

Emmylou fell promptly asleep on their stomach, and Bruno rested contentedly underneath the hammock as it swayed gently.

Chapter 2 Dani

Dani was going to kill Muir just as soon as she could stop the throbbing in her lower half, which she was afraid to look at. It would also be nice if her shoulder didn't feel quite so off. She didn't need her arms to swim, but her normally powerful merfolk tail wasn't working for her.

Of all the weeks in all the years, he chose now to pick a fight.

She'd always known her cousin was a total turd, but this was going way too far. As soon as she regained consciousness, she was going to kick his tailfin right back to the ocean. And speaking of losing consciousness, she was having more and more trouble keeping her eyes open.

That was going to be a problem if she couldn't get help soon.

Dani's swimming was sluggish, and she was having trouble moving her tail. Plus, all the oily blackness in the surrounding water was her own blood, as far as she could tell.

There was so much of it.

Her vision narrowed, the edges of her sight going black.

She wondered absently if she should double check her medical records later to make sure she was up to date on her tetanus shots. Though she hadn't seen what had cut her, she was pretty sure it had been an alive thing, and she wondered if there was a vaccine for rabies.

And if there was, whether she'd need it.

Her parents and the other older merfolk were pretty good about keeping track of those things though. Dani really wished they were with her right now so she wouldn't have to be in charge of all this mess.

Then she did blackout, and when she came to, it was on land.

This was not good. This was really bad.

This was much worse than waking up in the water.

She tried to open her eyes, but the sun was so blindingly bright, even though it was overcast, and her head throbbed every time she tried to move.

Dani really didn't want to die as some rando's trophy catch and wind up on an episode of *Lake Monsters*, destined to play on late-night reruns during cryptid week on the History Channel for all eternity sandwiched between *Ancient Aliens* and *Bigfoot Hunters*.

She groaned and tried to move, but she was so sore and so tired.

The sound of tires screeching to a stop near her and skidding on gravel let her know she had probably washed ashore on a parking area near the end of the lake. Where humans liked to park their RVs and walk across the dam and take lots of pictures.

She was hooked. This was going to be quite the way to go.

"Dani?" a familiar voice shouted.

It was Florence, and she was acting hysterical.

"Hmm, I would have thought I'd hallucinate Kye," Dani murmured under her breath. "Or Emmylou, I'd like her with me."

"Dani, oh my gawd, what happened?"

"If you're here to usher me into the next life, could you stop screeching?"

"I'm not screeching, and you're not dead, but oh no no no, what can I do to help you?"

"You are definitely screeching," Dani said, simultaneously realizing that maybe Florence wasn't in her head and also that she was about to pass out again.

Dani woke up rolled in a tarp that Florence was attempting to lift into the bed of her truck. Florence wasn't weak, but she also wasn't winning any weightlifting contests. Regardless, Dani was impressed at her tenacity and just how far she'd managed to drag her already.

"I'm too heavy, just leave me," Dani moaned. Her arm hurt so freaking bad. She just wanted to stay passed out and wallow in her pain, and why was Florence even bothering.

"Shut your mouth, Dani. I'm not leaving you here. You want some hick noodler to find you?" At the lack of response, Florence added, "I didn't think so."

Florence sat down suddenly, weak from the exertion. Dani could tell she had been crying. Her hands were shaking, and she was breathing rapidly.

"Aw, Florence, it'll be okay," Dani smiled weakly at her. "Stop being such a weenie."

"You're not even gonna be nice to me right now?" Florence said with a half-hearted laugh.

"Just giving you a little motivation."

Florence nodded and dusted off her hands. "Okay, I need you to stay awake for just a second, Dani. Then you can nap, just as soon as we get you into the truck bed."

Both of them looked up at the three-foot clearance they would need to surmount. It had never seemed tall before, especially since Florence would never do something like change the height of her classic '51 Chevy. Grateful that Florence was as much a hipster as a lake girl at heart, Dani nodded.

"I'm going to lift your tail if you can use your good arm to pull yourself up." Florence positioned herself near Dani's middle.

Dani nodded. "Count of three?"

Florence counted down, and they both heaved.

The last thing Dani remembered was the sound of Florence slamming the tailgate shut and saying, "Swear to me you won't die in my truck, Dani. You know how much I love this truck. Plus, think how mad Kye will be if we let that happen."

This was going to be fine, Dani thought.

And she blacked out again.

Chapter 3 Kye

"Ack, Florence, what is going on?" Kye was suddenly awoken from a frankly blissful nap to her yelling and shaking them out of the hammock. The music was blaring in their headphones, so it wasn't until she yanked them out of Kye's ears that the words "Dani" and "hurt" and "truck" registered and the sleepy nap fog cleared with a snap.

There were a few moments when Kye felt like their whole world was up in the air, moving in slow motion. Then they were running with Florence the few yards to the back of the truck where Dani lay wrapped in a tarp.

"Oh my gosh, is she breathing? Is she alive?" Kye asked, the panic rising like bile in their throat.

Florence put both her arms on Kye's shoulders. "Listen to me, Kye. She's breathing. She's alive. And I need you to be the calm one right now because she definitely needs our help and I am one step away from a full-blown and very well-deserved panic episode. So focus."

Kye took a shaky breath and nodded.

"Breath in. Breath out." Florence coached. They breathed together, and Kye wrapped her in a quick, fierce hug and then went into fix-it mode.

"We need to get her into water," Kye said.

"We're not taking her to her parents?"

"Even if we could risk them knowing about us, they're not home," Kye said. The merfolk were for sure supposed to be secret from humans, and though Kye was willing to risk Dani being grounded for life if her parents found out they knew about Dani and all the other merfolk, they weren't in town. They weren't even in the lake. "They're spawning upriver. It's the first time Dani and Muir got left in charge of the younger ones."

"Well dang! Are the rest of them okay?" Florence looked out at the lake.

"I have no idea. We need to find Muir or Billy probably. But right now, we need to focus on Dani and get her fixed up. If she wakes up, she can tell us what happened."

Florence nodded.

"Help me get the canoe from around back." Kye jumped into action.

Bruno, meanwhile, barely opened one eye at the commotion and only did so briefly when he realized Florence was not going to drop everything and give him scratches like she usually did. Emmylou remained asleep in the hammock where Kye had left her.

As quickly as they could, Kye and Florence dragged the canoe to the back deck and started filling it with water from the hose.

Then Kye directed Florence while she carefully backed the truck up as close to the canoe as she could. Kye wanted to make sure that whatever was wrong with Dani wasn't made worse by them dragging her along the decking.

Together, they lowered her as gently as they could, which wasn't easy because she was completely dead weight.

And slippery. At least on her bottom half.

Inelegant as it was though, they got her into the water and out of the tarp, which was soaked in oily, black blood.

Florence stifled a gag.

"You don't have to stay here to watch." Kye gave her a reassuring pat on the back. She had always been squeamish, and the fact that she'd gotten Dani this far and in this condition was no small miracle.

If Kye had believed in that sort of thing.

They watched Florence take a few deep breaths.

"No, I'm okay," she said. "Just tell me what you need. It's going to be dark soon. We need to hurry."

Kye could cry. Their best friend was possibly the best human on the entire earth.

"Could you get me the first aid kit?" Kye looked more closely at the gash in Dani's tail. "And my grandpa's tackle box."

It was probably only moments before Florence returned, but Kye took that time to whisper demands to Dani that she better stay alive and to give her a gentle kiss on the forehead. Dani's skin felt clammy, and there was a sheen of sweat across her brow. Her usually golden brown skin had lost its warm glow.

Florence quickly arrived back at the canoe with the supplies Kye had asked for. Kye took the tackle box and the first aid kit from her and opened both up on the picnic table they'd dragged over.

"Do you have a plan?" She watched with a grimace as Kye began laying out tools and bandages.

"Bleeding bad?" Kye shrugged. "Not bleeding better?"

"I mean, you're not wrong, but also, I really wish we could take her to a doctor," she said, worrying her hands. Kye knew they needed to get her focused on a task soon or her anxiety was going to lead to a panic attack.

"It's not much worse than when you cut your arm that summer on the fence." Kye tied their hair into a quick messy bun.

"Okay, but that was human skin, and we used human butterfly bandages. This is a lot different."

15

Florence tried her best to not look directly at the giant gash down Dani's fin.

"Same concept though." Kye snapped on some gloves and pulled back the towel they'd quickly wrapped around Dani's tail.

"Oh heavens, I'm gonna hurl." Florence gagged.

"Florence Elizabeth, don't you dare puke over here," Kye said sternly. "I think we need to pop her shoulder back into its socket before I start messing with her tail, and I'm gonna need your help."

Florence nodded. They'd actually done this together a few summers ago when they were swimming with some family. Kye's cousin Hal was constantly popping his out of its socket because of some genetic thing that made his joints all wobbly, and he taught everyone how to help him when he needed it popped back in.

It was decidedly more difficult with Dani being in the canoe, and she groaned when they lifted her up by her vest. But they counted, "One, two, three," and got the shoulder back in place.

It took them an embarrassing three tries, and Kye was even more grateful that Dani didn't wake up. They would not be telling her how inefficient that whole part was. Kye examined Dani's smooth brown skin and could see bruises forming on her shoulder and arm like she had been yanked.

Florence stood up a bit unsteadily and was clearly trying her best to look anywhere but at Dani.

Kye realized they were going to have to keep Florence out of the way for the next part. And they knew that when Florence was about to panic, clear direct orders were best. "Go inside, search online for anything about giving stitches to fish, and bring me some alcohol, please."

When Florence headed into the house, Kye gently poured filtered water they'd pulled from the garage over the gash that raked down Dani's tail. Several of the teal scales were ripped apart and turning gray. The edges where the cut was were curled and fading. When Kye touched them, they fell away like burnt edges of pages from a book. They gently brushed their hands along the cut, wiping away the decayed parts until the wound was open but cleaner.

Dani let out a groan but didn't seem to be in more pain than before, and she remained unconscious, only making small sounds while Kye worked.

They couldn't focus on it being Dani and just needed to stop the weeping, oily blood from flowing. It had significantly slowed, but Kye didn't know if that was from a lack of blood (bad) or from healing (good). There was no way to do a transfusion without tracking down another merfolk, and even then, that was some medieval medical shit to just be winging.

17

Florence came back as Kye was tying fishing line to the smallest hooks they could find.

"Here ya go." She handed them a bottle of whiskey.

Kye looked at it a beat then took it, uncapping it and taking a swig. They let out a cough and handed it back. "I meant rubbing alcohol but thanks."

"Oops, yeah that makes more sense." Florence glanced quickly at Dani then looked away again. "Also, the internet search was pretty much useless. Everything was just Etsy shops selling fish embroidery patterns."

"Who would want that?"

She shrugged. "I have no idea. There was also a really upsetting article about making stitches *from* fish guts."

"Eww," Kye muttered, continuing to prepare their own makeshift sutures with all the scraped-up confidence they could manage.

"After that, the internet pooped out, and now it's just pinwheel of doom central in there." She looked out at the setting sun. "It's gonna be dark soon,"

"I better get to work." Kye was determined to get Dani put back together.

It took about an hour, but Kye got the gash in Dani's tail sewn up. Kye assumed that bandages wouldn't have been much help since any adhesive would just come off as soon as Dani got back into the water, so Kye had used fishing line to sew her up. Lining up her scales perfectly was impossible since so many had fallen away, but Kye did their best to stitch her up in a way that hopefully wouldn't pull too much and hurt her swimming speed.

When they finished running over the whole wound with alcohol, Florence—who had spent much of the past hour rigging up a way to siphon off the water—helped them replace the murky water in the canoe with clean.

As soon as they finished filling it up, Bruno walked over with Emmylou on his head and rested his chin on the edge of the canoe so Emmylou could hop onto Dani's shoulder.

"Your pets are so weird," Florence said.

Kye nodded. They stood with a yawn and stretched but did not leave their spot by the canoe. "I'm gonna sleep out here."

"I'll bring you a sleeping bag and a sandwich." Florence squeezed Kye's shoulder. "And maybe a beer?"

"That sounds amazing."

Chapter 4 Kye

Kye woke up to their name being shouted from the water by dock.

It took them a second to realize what was happening. Then the whole night before flashed through their head, and they shot up, out of their sleeping bag.

"Kye, I need to talk to you!"

They let out a sigh of relief when they recognized the voice. It was just Billy, who they needed to talk to anyway.

"One second," they shouted back.

Leaning over Dani, they quickly checked to make sure she was sleeping soundly and that the stitches were still holding. Some of the bronze warmth had returned to her skin, and she actually looked really peaceful. Hopefully, that would be how she felt when she woke up. Pulling a tarp loosely over the canoe on the off chance that a neighbor wandered by, Kye slipped on their sandals and jogged down the wooden ramp to their boat dock.

Billy was there, wearing his ridiculous baseball cap backward, his black curls peeking out from underneath it. The expression on his face was one of someone feeling completely put out.

"Are you okay?" Kye was concerned that he might have been hurt by whatever it was that got Dani, though he wasn't showing any signs of that.

"Yes, I'm fine, but I'm ticked off!" he whined in his thick Oklahoma accent. "Is Dani with you? She's supposed to be in charge while our folks are all gone, and she's not around. I need a break from watching all these dang kids."

"Dani's hurt." Kye was confused and also now becoming annoyed at the thirteen-year-old. He always got annoying after a bit, but today he got there a lot quicker. Maybe it was Kye's lack of sleep. "She was in some accident. We thought you might know what happened."

"I don't know." Billy at least showed a slight bit of concern for his older third cousin once the 'hurt' part had registered. "She and Muir went off and didn't come back, and they were supposed to be taking care of us."

"Is Muir missing?" Kye asked, concern furrowing their brow.

"Yep, since last night," Billy said, exasperated. Kye was grateful that all their own cousins were older so they never had to deal with obnoxious young ones.

"Aren't you worried about them?" Kye asked, crossing their arms.

"I mean, yeah, but mostly I just wanna know what to do with the school."

"Well, Billy, you're gonna need to keep them safe until Dani wakes up or Muir comes back," Kye said, irritated. "We can't exactly bring them here because you know someone will tattle on us knowing about y'all."

"Is she hurt real bad?"

"Yeah, but I stitched her up."

"She needed stitches?" he asked, eyes wide. "What happened to her?"

"No idea." Kye sagged wearily against a post. "Florence found her down by the boat slip near the dam and brought her here. Her tail got cut, and her shoulder was out of socket. Now she's just sleeping really hard. She hasn't woken up once since she got here, but she was talking to Florence before."

Billy nodded. "She's probably in a winter's rest."

"What's that?"

"It's when we're really sick or hurt and kinda go into like a hibernation to get healed. It's called that because we also sorta slow down all winter, or at least we used to until we got heaters and stuff."

"Okay, that's good then? That she's resting?" Kye wished for not the first time that they had asked

Dani a lot more questions, rather than spend all their time together just goofing off.

"Yeah, for her but not for me. I'm tired of babysitting."

"Billy, it's really important that you keep yourself and the other kids safe, okay? We don't know what happened to Dani, and we're gonna have to go look for Muir. Come get us if you need, but probably just stick close to the lake house."

Billy nodded. "Okay fine." He started to swim away then popped back up to the surface and hollered. "Thanks for taking care of Dani."

That kid was such a pain. Kye hurried back up to the deck to check on Dani.

Florence was there with the largest plate of bacon and homemade biscuits that Kye had ever seen.

"I stress brunched." She shrugged and handed them a steaming cup of coffee.

"You are my best friend for countless reasons." Kye took the mug and the plate from her and sat back down on the sleeping bag next to the canoe. "But right now, the number one reason is this bacon."

"And cheesy eggs." She brought over a pan from the stove and pushed a huge pile onto Kye's plate.

Kye shoveled a few mouthfuls then filled Florence in on what Billy had said.

23

"One of us should go search for Muir. He might be hurt," Florence said, when Kye had finished recounting what he'd told them.

Neither of them was super keen on looking for him. He was kinda a dick, and though he and Florence had sort of dated in middle school, he always made it clear that he was superior to the rest of them because he was the oldest.

"I'll go," Florence offered. "You should keep an eye on Dani."

"That's okay. I'm faster in the boat. And as far as I can tell, Dani is doing good. Billy said this sleep thing is her healing. I'll go get changed and head out." Kye almost wanted Florence to argue with them about it so they could stay and watch over Dani, but it would likely just be watching her sleep and they didn't want to seem creepy.

After quickly finishing the rest of their breakfast and downing another cup of coffee, Kye swapped out their jean shorts for some windbreaker pants and a light waterproof jacket and got the boat uncovered. It was still so early in the year that no one was taking it out regularly, but it started right up.

They technically weren't supposed to take the boat out when their parents were out of town, but desperate times.

"Hop in, Bruno," Kye said, and the big dog lumbered onto the boat, taking his favorite spot on the bow and falling instantly asleep.

"Be safe," Florence said.

Kye gave her a thumbs-up, backing the boat out of the slip and heading out onto the lake. As soon as Kye steered out into the open water, the warmth of the deck left their hands and face. The lake was still frigid from the wintertime, and Kye was glad they'd opted for the dorky windbreaker pants because the spray from the boat was already getting them wet. The waters were choppier than usual too, especially for a day that didn't seem overly windy, though there were clouds forming on the horizon.

Kye took a path that led them past the lake house where Billy and hopefully the rest of the younger merfolk were hanging out, but they didn't steer too close, assuming Billy would let them know if Muir showed back up there.

It might have been better to wait for Dani to wake up. But Billy had acted like it might be a while, and if Muir was hurt, they needed to try and help.

Since Dani had washed up on the southern edge of the lake, near the dam, that was the direction Kye headed, scanning the shoreline for any signs of Muir as they went.

They'd taken the boat this way a thousand times but had almost always had a parent, or at least

Florence, with them. Often, it had been to meet up with Muir and Dani during summer months when they could sneak away long enough.

Kye was thinking about a particularly fun summer when they'd essentially taken over a small cove tucked away from sight and spent many days visiting them in the same spot. Each day they weren't caught emboldened them, and it wasn't until Billy had followed Muir and Dani that they'd been spotted. Fortunately for everyone, Billy could actually keep his mouth shut if given enough bribes. Dani and Muir had done his chores for months, until their parents caught on that something was up, and at that point, Billy had kept the secret too long to tattle without getting himself in trouble as well.

Their mind was still wandering when they spotted a group of people on a dock. Normally, that wouldn't be a big deal at all since gatherings on docks was a major part of lake life, but it was chilly out and they were all definitely wearing matching robes.

Brief thoughts of elves and hobbits crossed Kye's mind. For the shortest moment, they thought that maybe it was a group of LARPers.

Then they recognized the insignia on the wooden deck cover over the dock.

"What are these weirdos doing out here right now?" they muttered, planning on giving the Church of the Flood a wide berth and hopefully slipping past

26

unnoticed. But a flash of scales caught their eye. "What the deck?"

Muir was with them.

His body was stretched out on a long, wooden table, and he was positioned between several of the members of the church, who faced him. Even over the sound of the motor, Kye could tell they were chanting something.

Kye couldn't see his torso, but his tail was distinguishable.

Then one of the members lifted up a long spike, and it looked as though they were going to drive it into Muir's chest.

"No!" Kye shouted and steered the boat quickly to the dock.

It got the notice of the half dozen members, and as one, they turned toward Kye. The boat was almost to the dock, and Kye was filled with dread that Muir was already dead and they were about to find the filleted body of their childhood friend.

But then he sat up.

And gave Kye a wink.

Chapter 5 Dani

Dani willed her eyes to open, but it was so much more tempting to just go back to sleep. She wondered vaguely if Florence would be nice and get her a comforter or quilt to wrap up in.

Yes, quilts and duvets were an impractical thing for a merfolk to use because of general sogginess, but she'd felt enough on picnics to know it would be cozy. And cozy sleep seemed like the best idea.

But she shook herself awake again, groaning as she tried to sit up.

"Dani!" Florence knelt beside her and grabbed her shoulders, steadying her.

"Oww, hey." She tried to shrug Florence off but was finding it extremely difficult to move.

"I'm really glad you're awake. But you're fixin' to dislocate your shoulder again if you don't take it easy, and Kye's gonna kill me if they get back and you're hurt more."

Dani nodded but knew it was going to be harder to stay awake if she couldn't move around.

"I need to wake up," Dani muttered, eyes drooping.

"Billy said that your body is in like a special rest because you got so banged up, so rest is good."

The sound of Billy's name woke her up more. "Is Billy okay?"

"Yeah, he's fine. He was just here a while ago. What happened?" Florence helped Dani take a drink of ice water. After the first sip, she took the glass from Florence and gulped the rest of it down in just two swallows.

"Muir?" she gasped through her grogginess.

Florence looked down reflexively. "We don't know, but Kye went to go find him. I'm sure he's all right and they'll both be back soon."

"No," Dani croaked. "Muir did this."

"What do you mean?" Florence asked in shock. Dani loved Florence dearly, but she would have much preferred to have had Kye there instead so she didn't have to elaborate.

Her throat was raw from being out of the water for so long, and darling Florence was often so frantic she didn't slow down enough to read between lines. Whereas Kye appreciated terseness.

"Muir," Dani said, struggling to stay conscious. "He's the one who did this." Then, much to her frustration, she blacked out again.

Chapter 6 Kye

Kye eased the boat closer and, when Muir reached out his hand and beckoned them, pulled up close enough to the dock to toss a rope around a cleat.

"Kye, come." Muir gestured toward them with an open hand. "I want you to meet my friends."

This was all extremely weird, and while Kye was grateful that their friend seemed to be both alive and coherent, they were most definitely not keen on hopping onto that pier. But they did so anyway.

Bruno stayed on the boat and didn't wake up from his nap. Typical.

"Hi, everyone, I'm Kye." They introduced themself and stepped closer to the table Muir was sitting on.

"Oh, no need for that," Muir said brightly and with a smile that didn't quite reach his eyes. "They've all heard all about you, of course."

His peppiness was disconcerting.

"Oh, they have?" Kye looked around the group of half a dozen or so cloaked individuals. Each had on a floor-length robe emblazoned with Church of the Flood insignia. They were not exactly forthcoming with the greetings. "Well, folks, I suppose that puts me at a disadvantage."

Still, they said nothing, and Kye wondered if they could speak, even if they wanted to. Kye did recognize the younger one from the grocery store the other day, but there was no indication that they recognized Kye.

"Kye, my dear Kye." Muir stretched out his hands to take theirs in his. "I'm so sorry the rest of our friends just couldn't see the benefits of what we're trying to accomplish. I'm so glad you're here."

As Muir pulled them a step closer together, Kye gulped in a way that they were really hoping wasn't audible. Ignoring that comment and the half dozen strangers surrounding them, Kye took a moment to look Muir up and down.

"New ink?" they asked.

It was an understatement.

Muir had been mid tattoo when they'd shown up, and half of his chest was newly covered with black designs.

"Looks a tad white-frat-boy-tribal, even for you." Kye tried to pull their hands back, but Muir held on tighter.

He chuckled softly. "Oh, Kye, not you too."

"Not what me?" they asked, this time yanking their hands away. Glad that Muir let go, they took a step backward.

"Are you going to tell me that my ideas are those of a lunatic also?"

"Really don't know what you're talking about, dude. I just came here to check on my friend."

A short, scowling woman spoke up from beneath her hood. "The chosen one does not need you to know what he is talking about."

"See, like I said," Muir began.

"Muir, I have no idea—"

A second robed stranger chimed in. "You do not interrupt the chosen one."

Muir held up a hand. "No, it's okay, I've got this."

He pushed himself forward on the table so he was as close to Kye as his position would allow, looking them right in the eye.

"Muir," Kye started again in a hushed voice, though they knew that even whispering the others would be able to hear. "I truly have no idea what you're talking about, but I'm pretty sure these folks are bad news and if you want to come home with me, we can do that. Right now. Dani is waiting. Billy and the rest of the school are okay. Let's just go. No harm done."

At that last line, he scoffed, and Kye knew with a sinking feeling in their stomach that harm was about to be done if it hadn't already.

"No harm done?" he said sarcastically. His black eyes widened then narrowed, and the other people hissed.

They literally hissed.

"No. Harm. Done?" This time he yelled.

Kye took another step back, but now they were on the edge of the dock and held up their hands. "I'm just trying to understand what is happening."

"It's been happening, Kye, and you know it." Muir scowled and crossed his arms. "Just look around you."

Kye didn't really feel like turning their back to anyone currently present, so went with peripheral vision to accommodate this demand.

"It's been happening," he repeated, "And we are finally going to do something about it."

"Oh yeah." Kye desperately wanted to step back even further even if it meant a cold plunge into the lake. "What is it you're going to do?"

"Bring it all down." He gestured to the lake with a wide grin.

"Really going to need you to be more specific."

"The dam," he grinned wickedly. The dude had always been kinda sleazy in Kye's opinion, but this look on him was extra slimy. It amazed them that Muir and Dani were related, even if it was super distantly. "It will be the start to a flood that will cover all of the earth."

"Well, that is an exceedingly foolish idea." Kye's eyes widened. Muir was ballsy, but this was going to take the whole audacity cake.

"It's my job to protect these lands."

"Protect?" Kye scoffed. "Do you have any idea the destruction that would cause? The devastation?"

Muir shook his head. "I thought you of all people would understand."

"I truly apologize for ever giving you that impression." Kye's hand found its way to a life hook hung on the pillar where they stood.

"If you won't join us, I can't let you stop me either." Muir snarled and clenched his fists. "The planet needs cleansed, and we will be the ones to cleanse it."

"Right, so, I'm gonna go ahead and go." Kye grasped the pole and swung it between themself and Muir as he reached forward to grab at them.

"We can't let that happen." One of the rando cultists hissed.

As the group of them stepped forward, Kye jabbed Muir right in the chest where his new tattoos were still bleeding. He yelped, and the cultists turned toward him in concern, giving Kye enough time to hop onto the boat.

"Get them," Muir shouted, pointing to Kye.

It took a few heart-pounding moments to get the boat started, but Bruno luckily had chosen to bother and was baring his teeth at the people, who now hesitated to hop onto the boat after them.

Bruno's temporary ferociousness gave Kye enough time to turn the boat around and push it full throttled into the lake.

A quick glance behind them showed Muir had jumped into the water and was already gaining on them and quickly. His powerful tail propelled him through the water until he was caught up with their wake. Then he was pulling up alongside the boat.

Kye had never had to steer the boat evasively and was grateful that Bruno was steady on his feet as they swerved away from Muir.

They were almost to their home, and if they could manage to get onto land, Muir would be slowed down significantly.

But they didn't have to wait for that.

Around fifty yards from the dock, from the corner of their eye, they saw Muir stop abruptly. With a shout, he slammed into what looked like nothing.

Looking back, Kye could see that the water where Muir had halted seemed to be churning angrily as though against a seawall. The same feeling of safety enveloped them as usual, but now, it was more distinct. When Kye looked closer, the air crackled with something that blocked Muir from getting any further.

Maybe that protective feeling they always got when they came home was more than just familiarity.

Regardless, they shut off the boat and hopped out quickly, whistling for Bruno to follow, and ran up the ramp to the porch, whispering a grateful word to whatever had stopped Muir. Before they went inside, Kye looked out at the water, where they could still see him at the barrier, pacing.

Kye rushed up the ramp, where Florence was waiting for them at the top.

"Oh my gosh, Kye, are you okay?" She took them by the shoulders and then wrapped them into a hug.

"I think so?" They hugged Florence back for a few moments then pulled away. "Is Dani awake yet?"

The two of them went over to where Dani rested in the canoe.

"Not quite," Florence said, "but she keeps waking up more frequently. She said Muir was the one who attacked her. Did you find him?"

Kye nodded grimly. "Yeah, he did it. And I get the sense that it's all about to get way worse."

After Kye quickly filled her in on what had happened at the Church of the Flood's dock and then again as they drove the boat back, the two of them grabbed a couple of sandwiches from the kitchen and sat next to Dani. Bruno had lumbered on up and was patiently pretending to sleep until Kye was ready to offer him the crust of their sandwich.

36

"That is wild." Florence took a bite of her sandwich once Kye had finished adding more details of anything they could remember to their account. "Are we sure those cult folks won't come here?"

"I have no idea. Whatever it was that kept Muir from coming to the dock, might not be on the land too? But we do have SimpliSafe." Kye wasn't sure if they'd actually set the alarm though and hopped up to check it. When they got back, they added, "Plus, Bruno is a good guard doggo."

Kye scratched him behind the ears, and he didn't even open an eye.

Dani opened her eyes a crack. "If Bruno's a good guard dog, then Emmylou is a great chef."

Chapter 7 Dani

"You're awake!" Florence handed Dani a cup of water.

"Kye, are you okay?" Dani took the water and then held out her other hand to Kye.

"Yeah, I'm okay, I'm here." Kye looked at her intently like she might break. "I'm gonna pretend you didn't just imply my dog isn't a good guard dog, just because I'm so glad you are awake."

"Florence said you went to find Muir." Her eyes drooped, and she looked like she might fall asleep again. But she sat up with grunt and squeezed Kye's hand.

Dani tried to focus on the conversation, but Kye absentmindedly ran their thumb over the line of small scales that ran down the back of her hand.

"Yes." Kye cleared their throat. "He seems to have pretty much lost his dang mind?"

Dani nodded. "That's the impression I got too."

"I think you're safe here though. It seems like Muir can't swim any closer." Kye said they had watched him swimming laps back and forth for a quarter of an hour, before he disappeared beneath the surface. They hadn't seen him again since.

Dani wasn't sure what could keep him from swimming to the dock, but hoped that whatever it was, it would hold until they had a plan. She groaned and sat up further. "I need to check on Billy and the kids."

"Billy is supposed to swing back by in an hour." Florence had called their landline, and he'd picked up. "They're hanging out at the lake house, and so far, Muir hasn't messed with them."

Dani nodded. "It would be good for me to get into the actual lake water if you think it's safe."

She wasn't used to feeling so extremely vulnerable and unsure, and she kinda hated it.

But Kye stood. "I'll come with you."

"Me too." Florence dusted off her shorts. "Want us to give you a push? I could grab the wheelbarrow."

"Oh my kraken, what happened while I was unconscious?" Dani grimaced.

"We'll fill you in on all the gruesome details." Kye took Dani's elbow and helped her out of the canoe.

"And no, I do not want a push." Dani rolled her eyes and made her way down the ramp.

"Be careful of your cut," Kye said. "I'm suddenly very worried about splinters in fins and what taking those out would cost me emotionally."

Dani made her way to the dock, and it was not lost on her that merfolk on land were super awkward. Like floppy juvenile elephant seals. There was so much flopping, and yet, Dani couldn't care less. Though halfway down the ramp she was almost wishing she'd taken Florence up on her offer of a wagon ride.

But it was well worth the trek when she reached the cool water and dove in.

Surfacing with a contented sigh, her tail was already feeling stronger than it had up on the deck. The stitches were tight, and she could feel them pulling when she tried to turn certain directions, but it felt rejuvenating to stretch out. Her shoulder still ached, and she didn't want to over-work it yet. So, she took a few strokes then let her tail do most of the work.

Dani swam in a few circles then came back to the dock, where Kye was pulling up two porch chairs. Bruno took a spot within scratching distance of all of them. Emmylou followed closely and plunked into the water. She swam a few plump circles then came to a rest on Dani's tail.

Every once in awhile Kye would find a dead June bug wedged between the wooden slats and Dani would lift the end of her fin out of the water, so Emmylou could eat the treat out of their hand.

Florence appeared soon after with a three cans of low-point beer and coozies for them all. As well as several more sandwiches. Where Florence was constantly pulling sandwiches from, Dani would never know. It was a very handy trait in a best friend, however, and both Kye and Dani were famished.

"Cheers." Kye took a sip of their beer.

Kye filled Dani in on what had happened with Muir and the things he had said. Then Dani did the same, though other than remembering an argument with Muir, most of what he said was fuzzy in her memory. She was worried she might have a concussion, but Florence assured her they'd checked for any bumps on her noggin. She did remember Muir spouting off about floods and cleansing, and it was all very distressing.

"We always knew Muir was gonna do something bonkers, but I didn't think he'd turn so violent." Florence shook her head sadly.

"None of us could have predicted he'd join a cult and do who-knows-what with them." Kye put their hand on Florence's shoulder, giving it a squeeze. Dani wondered if Kye had a deck chair big enough for her handy.

Florence leaned her head on Kye's shoulder, and Dani guessed that somehow Florence would equate this situation with something she'd done wrong in a decade's expired relationship. There was a time when Muir was close to them all, but Florence especially.

"This is why I'm treasurer for that Environmental Student Union Club." Florence sniffled. "So I can make a difference without, like, being a jerk about it."

"I'm sure you're a very good treasurer," Dani said. And Kye gave her a look, but Dani couldn't help it if she sometimes came across as sarcastic accidentally. "I mean it," Dani added. "It's good that you're doing good."

Florence's heart was constantly at end-of-the-book Grinch size.

"Though I don't really get the impression that these folks are so much worried about the environment as they want to wipe out all the land with a giant flood." Kye grimaced and took another sip of beer.

"Well, technically, if they wait another decade or two, most of it's gonna flood anyway," Florence said with another sniffle.

They all munched on the three types of sandwiches that Florence had whipped up, and if she closed her eyes, Dani could almost imagine it was the day she and Kye and Florence had planned.

Billy came by a few minutes later.

"Hey, Dani, you all right?" he asked, tugging on his baseball cap.

"Yeah, I'll be okay." Dani looked at the hat. "Wait, that's Muir's hat. He's gonna be so ticked you took it on top of all this."

"He's being a total dweeb right now, so I don't really care. Plus, you two were supposed to be in charge till the adults get back, and yet you're here drinking beer with your pals and ditching me." Billy huffed and crossed his arms.

Dani rolled her eyes at the kid. "I didn't ditch you. I was unconscious, and Muir is dangerous. We need to keep the school safe."

"How are you gonna do that?" Billy asked, clearly wanting nothing to do with the responsibility.

Bruno woke up and ambled close to Billy, who grinned and gave him a scratch. Billy slipped beneath the water and emerged a minute later with a crawfish in his outstretched hand. "Here, Bruno. Come here, good boy."

Bruno, who had already seemed to be asleep again in the short time it took Billy to find him a treat, opened one eye, then belly crawled until he was nose to nose with Billy, who held out his hand so Bruno could crunch down on the snack.

"I just need a little more rest," Dani said. "Okay?"

He scowled but nodded.

"Can I see it?" He nodded toward her tail, which she lifted to float on the surface. After studying it for a moment, his only comment was. "Metal."

"Just please watch the school tonight, Billy. I'll be by in the morning with a plan, and you can help me with it, possibly."

"Maybe, but there's a game on, so we'll have to see." Billy was being purposefully bratty, and Dani was briefly envious of her human friends who'd grown up so far from their neighbors and distant relatives. Even though Dani and Billy were only distantly related, the merfolk functioned like a big family a lot of the time, and he was practically a brother. And a total pain in the fins.

"Can you handle everyone tonight?" she asked.

He nodded. "Yeah, but you're gonna owe me."

"Sure. And Billy, if anything scary or weird happens, please call us. And don't trust Muir."

"Roger that." He took off as quickly as he'd popped in.

"That kid doesn't get enough discipline." Dani shook her head.

"Pretty typical for a teenager." Florence shrugged.

"We're all teenagers too." Kye pointed out.

The three of them took it easy for the next couple of hours. Mulling over ideas of what Muir's plans with the Church of the Flood might be, and after some discussion, Dani decided that visiting Grandmerm Sarnas was her best bet at getting help

44

from a merfolk elder since everyone else she knew was gone.

"She's an older river merfolk I went to visit with my folks when I was much younger," Dani explained as they shared a bag of chips, the sun beginning to set.

"Do you think she can help?" Florence asked.

Dani shrugged. "I'm not sure. But it's way too far for me to try and get to my folks without having to take all the school with me, and it might be weeks before they're back."

"So, what's she like?" Kye asked as Florence yawned.

"She was here even before my folks came. I know she's got a lot of knowledge about the area and stuff, but the last time I visited her was when I was, like, three so who knows." Dani wished she had a more concrete plan or a frigging cell phone that worked out there, but it wasn't like her parents could answer right then anyway.

"Would it be faster for us to drive you in Florence's truck?" Kye suggested.

Dani shook her head. "No, it's definitely one of those insiders-only situations. I think she'd hear the truck coming a mile away and get skittish. Plus, I need to go get directions anyway, and I doubt the parents left road maps."

45

"Well, let us know if there's anything you need." Florence tried unsuccessfully to stifle another yawn. "Do you want to sleep up at the house?"

Dani shook her head. "I'll be fine down here. That canoe was making my neck really stiff."

"Of course," Kye said. "Whatever is best for you."

"Well, I, for one, am sleeping in a bed." Florence stood and took her chair and the pile of sandwich plates with her.

Kye popped open another beer and handed it to Dani, moving from the deck chair to dangle their legs in the still, cool water off the deck. "I'll be up later."

"Thanks." She took a sip and set her bottle on the edge of the dock.

"No problem." Kye took more than a sip.

She noticed. "You okay?"

Kye nodded, but to her, it seemed stilted. They looked at her so earnestly and asked, "How about you?"

"I'm okay." Dani wanted to reassure Kye that she was fine and whatever was happening with her douche canoe of a third cousin would be over soon.

"Are you sure?" Kye asked, their voice cracking just slightly.

At the sound, she moved forward, putting her hand around their ankle where it rested under the water and giving it a gentle squeeze.

46

"Yes." She pulled herself a fraction of an inch closer then released her grip on their leg. "I have super merfolk healing powers. See? I'll prove it."

She dove into the waters and propelled herself up in a twisting arch that would have landed her on any USA Olympics swimming team, were the slight issue of her having a tail ignored.

"Okay, fine, fine." Kye laughed and grinned lopsidedly at her. "Please don't pull your stitches out reassuring me."

"Whatever it takes to get you to relax." Dani laughed and swam to rest her head on the dock.

"We should get some sleep." Kye finished their beer but made no move to go.

"After you." Dani, feeling exhausted, grinned up at them.

Chapter 8 Kye

Despite climbing into bed after most of the night had passed, Kye felt relatively refreshed and rode their bike to Dani's merfolk community lake house. Dani needed a few things wasn't sure if she had a wet bag and wanted to be able to keep from making multiple trips. So Kye, much to their growing curiosity, tagged along in case Dani needed help with any electronics or books.

Kye waited on the front porch while Dani shooed the kids and Billy out the back and into the lake. They couldn't help but notice just how "lake life" the front porch was. The door was painted a bright blue and sported a seashell wreath, complete with a white wooden anchor and fish cut-outs, and there was a white wicker bench holding have a dozen nautical themed pillows.

It wasn't Kye's style, but it was definitely charming.

Dani made her way to the front door and opened it up for Kye when they got there. They'd never been inside the lake house because of the whole "keeping their friendship secret from the merfolk parents" thing.

Kye couldn't hide their surprise when they looked around the living room.

It looked like a house straight from a lake house magazine cover.

"Why are there so many throw pillows?" Kye asked, looking at the couch and giant armchair set by the bay windows.

"The families started renting it out as a vacation getaway," Dani explained, making her way down to the second set of rooms at the back of the house. None of the merfolk slept there, but they all had some space to store things that needed to be kept dry, like tablets and laptops or, in Billy's case, baseball cards.

From the floor up, everything looked basically like a normal lake house. The floors, however, did not. Everything was either tile or sealed cement, and the places where there was wood had what looked like a Slip 'N Slide material covering it.

So the merfolk could slide.

It was not majestic, and Kye stifled a laugh after Dani shot them a look.

But it was so silly, and they couldn't help it. "What? It just looks like fun is all." Kye quickly changed the subject. "Is there any way at all to contact your folks?"

Dani shook her head. "Not while they're spawning. They won't be back for a couple weeks, and it would take so long to reach them. If it didn't seem like Muir was in such a rush, I'd take the school and head that way now."

She led the way to the back of the house and explained to Kye that it was locked off when people came to stay as guests. It was listed as a partial home on Air BnB, but they always cleared out when visitors came to stay, rolling up the tarps that kept their scales from catching on the wood, as a way of maintaining secrecy.

"What are we looking for?" Kye asked. Dani went to the low desk, opening up the laptop that she shared with her family.

"I need to get the key to the vault, and while we're here, we may as well look through Muir's stuff in case there's anything useful." Dani focused on logging into the laptop, so Kye took the time to look around.

They'd never gotten to look at Dani's space in the lake house and couldn't help but be curious. "Maybe something about the Church of the Flood?"

Dani nodded to a trunk. "You can look through Muir's stuff. I've got to check some things online."

Kye knelt down and opened up the trunk. It was mostly full of old bass fishing magazines, and a few novels were shoved at the bottom. And hair gel. Like, a lot of hair gel. "New theory, all this gel has made it impossible for him to think clearly, and that's what's caused him to totally lose it."

"Yeah, that might be good," Dani said, absently, clearly not listening. She let out an excited breath. She was trying to contain it, but Kye was watching her closely.

"What's up?" Kye asked.

"Um, I just got my GED?" Dani said.

"What!" Kye shrieked.

"Shh, it's not a big deal." But the excitement in her eyes betrayed her nonchalance.

"Whatever. We're celebrating tonight. Who cares about all this mess?" Kye said, scooting over and giving Dani a hug.

Dani seemed taken a bit by surprise but hugged them back after a beat.

"How did you even pull it off?" Kye asked.

She smirked. "The whole pandemic thing forced so much online so fast that I was able to slip in. Been taking the classes for the past two years."

"You are amazing." Kye hugged her tightly.

They broke apart, and Kye went back to searching through Muir's things, but it didn't seem to go anywhere, until they noticed a thick book tucked between a basketball jersey and a knit sweater.

Pulling it out and flipping to a random page, they let out an "Uh oh."

"What is it?" Dani leaned over to see what Kye had found.

It was definitely a scrapbook about the Church of the Flood.

"Looks like Muir is really into doodling about that cult and he has a lot of his own ideas too." Kye handed the book to Dani with a grimace. This was definitely weirder than the year Kye and Florence had made a scrapbook about the new Spider-Man movie.

There were pages full of scribbled cat-scratch writing, sometimes of the same word over and over again. Some of the pages had truly remarkable drawings of the Church of the Flood's building and of Muir himself.

The clippings from the church brochures were the weirdest part. He'd actually taken the time to cut out sections with pictures and glue them in then added little sticker photo frames on the edges, and, at some point, he'd used what looked like an entire sheet of coral reef themed stickers.

Kye couldn't decide if the weirdest part was the maniacal black pen scribbles or the part straight off of planner-gram.

They thought to themself for not the first time that day that having to live in a community with Muir was a total pain in the scales and they really felt sorry for Dani about it. Billy too for that matter.

They were also not looking forward to showing Florence the scrapbook. Having an odd ex in one's past is fine, but this was several levels of unhinged past odd.

"Take that, and I'll grab my laptop. Then let's head back to your place," Dani said. "The kids are going to get curious soon, and halftime is almost over so Billy won't be any help." She also grabbed her MP3 player. "And take this," she handed it to Kye. "I can't listen to Florence's playlist anymore."

"It really is way too cheerful for this whole situation, isn't it," Kye agreed with a chuckle, adding the player to their backpack.

On their way out, Dani grabbed a set of keys from a desk in another room. "I have to make a quick stop and make sure Billy is settled. The map I need is in our vaults. I'll meet you back at your place."

Kye nodded and hopped on their bike. They wished they could go with Dani, but it wasn't like they could suddenly breathe underwater.

And besides, they had another stop to make too.

The ride to the dam authority office was less than twenty minutes, and Kye didn't bother locking up their bike when they went up to the entry of the small building.

Most of the dam was controlled by a large center on the other side of the lake, but Kye knew from a tour they'd taken as a middle schooler that security there was really tight. Even if they let Kye in, the chances of getting to actually speak to someone who could help was slim. Instead, they bypassed that part and went to the office where they knew someone worked twenty-four hours a day to keep an eye on things. If anyone was going to notice damage happening to the dam, it should be that worker, and Kye was hopeful they'd listen.

That hope was dashed.

Almost immediately.

The man who opened the door was extremely well groomed and not wearing the typical uniform Kye was used to seeing.

"Hi, do you have a minute to talk?" Kye wasn't totally sure what they were going to say, but something along the lines of "there's a cult that has bad plans for the dam. Help please."

"I doubt it." They began to close the door, but Kye stuck their shoe in the way.

"It'll only take a second." But that was when Kye noticed the tattoos along the man's wrists, peeking out from his sleeves. They bore a striking resemblance to the fresh ones Muir had just gotten. "Actually, on second thought. Never mind. It's not a big deal. And you must be so busy."

He looked at Kye with narrowed eyes and took a step forward. Kye worried for a second that he was going to stop them from leaving.

A Mean Piece of Water

But he just said, "Well go on then."

Didn't have to tell them three times. They hopped on their bike and headed home.

Bruno trotted alongside the bike as they approached the boundary to Kye's land, and Kye was grateful for his company on the last leg of this ride.

Kye paid closer attention while approaching their land this time and could feel the subtle change in the air as they passed through. There was definitely something protecting them, and they let out a breath they hadn't realized they'd been holding.

Chapter 9 Dani

Dani swam cautiously to the underwater vault where the merfolk in Lake Hobotnica kept their most important documents. She couldn't think of a reason Muir would be there but really didn't want to be surprised by him if he was.

The vault was a major part of her community. Things like family histories and maps and old photograph collections were stored there. Anything they still didn't trust to the land. Though now Dani was worried that whatever the Church of the Flood had planned might damage their records.

Upon reaching a certain age, the merfolk were allowed access to it, though Dani suspected her own parents had rushed her initiation because they wanted her to scan in all the pages to make them available digitally, which she was slowly chipping away at. The works and histories had been copied onto waterproof paper that could be taken in and out of water and were also slowly being turned into digital archives. Though the merfolk a few generations back worried that opening their society to the evils of technology would be their downfall.

Dani thought this was ridiculous and the only way any of them could hope to survive and remain hidden was to keep on top of the technological advances of the day. Which was why she was so glad they lived in a time with the internet and that the grown merfolk in the lake had bought the lake house a generation back before the housing bubble made it next to impossible to do so without credit history. It meant they had an actual address, and the rest of them had grown fond of streaming services and mail delivery.

Having internet and shipping opened them up to revenue streams in the human realm as well, like day trading and online shops.

But for now, she needed to go to the physical location of the vault and pay extra attention to her surroundings, hoping to not run into Muir before she found what she needed.

Unsurprisingly, none of what was covered in merfolk training had made it into her GED requirements. She hadn't told even her family about getting her GED because she was worried they'd laugh or, even worse, make a big fuss. The argument, "What do we need to learn what humans think is most important for? We're merfolk," was actually valid but still annoying, especially since so much of their worlds overlapped now.

Using the key she'd picked up at the land house, Dani opened up the lock and swam through a small opening under the water and into a long, narrow tunnel, which was lined with shelves on both sides, as well as lanterns encased in glass that could be lit under the water. She carefully pulled the door shut behind her because the last thing she wanted was to be cornered in the small space.

She didn't bother with the lamps and just clicked on the battery-powered track lighting that had been installed months before.

Having a reliable shipping address had truly revolutionized underwater lake life.

Dani went straight for the river maps and found the one giving directions to Grandmerm Sarnas. A copy had been made from the original onto waterproof vellum, which was a relief. Taking the original would have been much more nerve wracking. Not everything in the vaults was priceless, but Dani didn't want to lose anything precious.

She studied it for a few minutes, making sure it was the correct one, and was glad to see she was familiar with the mouth of the river that it led her to. Then she looked through the occult and cult books, hoping to find something to help them discover more about the Church of the Flood: *Secret Societies of the Rural Midwest*, *The Cryptids of Keystone*, and

Someone Saw Something: Monsters in Midwest Lakes.

What they really needed was to get someone into their next church service, Dani thought, adding that to her ongoing list of things to run by Kye and Florence. Then, as a totally not Kye-related afterthought, Dani also grabbed a slim book of poems that Kye might like.

Feeling bold, Dani decided to stop by a few places on the way back to Kye's.

It was risky and she really hoped she wouldn't run into Muir, but she needed some supplies and didn't think they could wait. Plus, if Muir was looking for her, it would be at her room where she slept and kept her things, not the medical area where the merfolk kept a stock of medications and supplies.

The coast appeared clear when she swam to the small clinic area and quickly scanned the shelves. Individual family units kept their own daily medicine, of course, but during the spawning season, all the meds were kept in a more central location. It was also where there was a clinic set up for the times when a merfolk needed medical attention. Usually, it was for something minor like a snag on a fishing line or a snake bite.

Once, Billy had gotten a concussion when some boater had accidentally dropped a six pack of beer and it happened to hit his head. Muir and Dani had absconded with the Coors after they swam him to the clinic.

It was closer to the center of the lake than most of their sleeping areas so that all the families were within ten miles or so of it at any given time. Some families preferred to be closer inland, while others enjoyed the deeper parts of the lake where sunlight almost never reached. Dani's family was one of the more social ones, and so they slept in part of one of the old towns that had been demolished when the dam was built. Several families took up residence there, living less than a mile from one another, which was quite close by merfolk standards.

Like most of the merfolk structures, the clinic walls were made of porous netting that allowed water to flow freely but gave them walls and places to store items that might otherwise just float away. Years before, everything was kept in trunks, but the flexibility of the webbing wall systems was much more efficient. Privacy was rarely needed in merfolk life, and the constant movement of water was much easier to manage when structures let the water flow freely.

It also came in handy every time someone built a new dock or boat slip because moving things around was quick when everything was nets and tubing.

Some of the older merfolk still kept things in trunks out of nostalgia. But even those had been upgraded by the younger ones who were able to share the invention of much more durable materials. The first time Dani had shown her mom the Container Store website, it was like the angels in heaven started playing their trumpets just for them.

Because the clinic was always well-kept, she found what she was looking for quickly. Making sure to close up after herself, Dani took the supplies and made a stop at the land house.

"Hey, Billy." Dani bumped into him on the dock and didn't even have to go inside the house. He was playing a video game and flipping his tail in the water while two littles held on and bounced around.

"One sec." Based on the music, he was finishing up a track on Mario Kart.

While she waited, Dani took a few deep breaths. She reminded herself that she loved this kid. It was fine.

When the all-too-familiar sound of the end of the race happened, the two little ones yelled, "Dibs!" at the same time.

Billy held up a finger. "You each get a turn, but it's Malcolm's turn first." The other began to protest. "Uh uh. If you fight about it, I do another circuit."

Dani was impressed at how quickly they got in line.

"Good job, Billy." She pulled out the bag with the meds.

"Are these for Ellie and Sewah?" He took the bag from her, and she nodded. "Thanks. They need it. Ellie has been sneezing like forty-five times an hour, and it's so obnoxious."

"Well, they don't have to stay on land," she pointed out.

"They know, but everyone is watching a Gilligan's Island marathon on Nick at Nite and taking turns doing commentary, and they don't want left out." Billy shrugged.

Most merfolk didn't have to deal with seasonal allergies, given that they spent so much time in the water where the main irritants were oils and garbage. But as younger ones spent more and more time on land, allergies were becoming an issue.

The other medicine was for Sewah, who had an infection on her arm from getting bitten by a snapping turtle while they were messing with noddlers. Nothing serious, but she needed some antibiotics.

"I'll be back as soon as I can, Billy, I promise." Dani finished tying up her bag and gave him a hug. "And if you need anything, call Kye's house, okay?"

He nodded and hugged her back. "I gotta get inside. The commentary is getting pretty heated in there."

Dani dove back in the water and hurried to Kye's.

She met Kye and Florence on the dock, and the three of them had her gathered resources spread across the wood.

Dani was looking over the map of the rivers, and she'd also gotten a couple other maps of the lake at various historical moments, while Kye thumbed through the poetry book and Florence looked over a map of the town before it was dismantled and cleared out to make way for the dam project.

"What's that?" Florence asked, looking closer. Just outside of the main town, there was a large structure labeled Ecclesia Inundatio.

"I think it's Latin." Kye tilted their head and studied it with Florence.

"Church Flood." Dani surprised even herself with that.

"I thought that church was really new," Kye said.

"Apparently not." Dani examined the map where Florence pointed. "I know that area though. It's just a foundation, like most of the human structures from the town before. Nothing special about it except it's big. Probably swam past it a hundred times."

"So, no indication that it was a church?" Florence asked.

Dani shook her head. "No, but that's not unusual. Construction materials were so expensive when the dam was built that they saved pretty much every piece they could and hauled it off to other towns. If that was a location of the Church of the Flood, it wouldn't surprise me if they'd moved any crosses or things to their new location."

"Think we should check it out?" Kye had that serious eye crinkle face that let Dani know they didn't really like an idea that they themself had.

"I mean, yeah, I think I should." Dani sort of wished she'd just gone that way when she'd made the trip to get the medicine, but no such luck.

"Could you a least take Billy with you?" Kye asked.

"He might not be very helpful." Dani shrugged.

"But it'll make us feel better." Florence glanced between the two of them and the churning waters.

"Okay, but y'all have to figure out a bribe for me to give him. And we may have to get some pizzas delivered to the land house."

"That's gonna cost a fortune," Florence pointed out, so they ditched that idea and stuck with bribing Billy directly.

Dani truly had not known what she expected to see when she and Billy got to the old foundation. But what was there was a giant gaping hole that should not have been there and had definitely never been there before.

"Well, silt," she muttered.

"That's new," Billy said.

"Does it look like something is inside of it?" she asked, mostly to herself, subconsciously taking a stroke back away from the hole.

In the depths of the hole there was the slightest purple glow. The longer they looked over the edge, the more distinct it was. A dome, shining subtly in the deep. Purple and blue and slowly pulsing like a heartbeat.

"This is really, really bad," Dani whispered. "We should go."

Billy nodded slowly, listening to her for once, and they edged away from the opening, trying not to disturb the water. Once they were clear of the hole, they picked up speed.

"We've got to go to our folks and warn them," he said.

And Dani wanted to, but there wasn't time.

"We'll never make it upstream that far in time to stop whatever is happening," she said. "He must have planned this for when they were spawning. So they wouldn't be here to interfere."

"Muir sucks." Billy too pulled back, looking around.

She nodded. "I'm going straight to Sarnas now. Hopefully she will tell us what to do."

"Want me to go with you?"

Dani shook her head. "I need to travel fast and know that you're watching the school. And if anything happens, you need to contact Kye or Florence."

He nodded, but before he split off from her, he held out his hand. She thought he was going in for a hug.

But he just wanted the pack of baseball cards. Because he was a total pain in the tail.

Chapter 10 Dani

Dani set off for Grandmerm Sarnas as soon as she updated Kye and Florence on what she and Billy had seen. She wanted to get a start on the swim since she was going to have quite a distance to cover if she wanted to make it back by the evening and the afternoon was quickly moving along. She could swim in the dark just fine but was rightfully jumpy about whatever had attacked her.

She left Emmylou Harris with Kye and Florence and swam past her own lake house to make sure that Billy and the kids were settled, even though she had just been over there. Going to see Sarnas was the best idea they had, but she still felt guilty leaving the school without her.

Kye and Florence had offered to have them all come to Kye's family's house, but they could pretty much take care of themselves. Plus, the secrecy codes were already being torn to bits. If she could keep any of the little kids from being involved, that was for the best.

So, Dani left after a few minutes and made sure Billy knew there were plenty more baseball cards in his future if he kept them wrangled.

His primary response was a shrug and to say, "After *Gilligan's Island*, there's a *This Old House* marathon on that everyone is into, so it should be fine."

"Okay, just don't let Fox try and check for veneers again." It had turned out that most of the wooden furniture in the lake home was solid, but one can still destroy an antique checking to confirm.

He rolled his eyes. "Obviously. I don't want to be grounded."

She had a bag packed with the map in case she got lost, as well as some snacks and an offering for the Grandmerm. Though Dani was too young to remember the one time her parents had taken her to meet the elder with much specificity, she did recall her folks presented Sarnas with tokens of appreciation when they visited.

Having almost no idea what that might entail, Dani had gone with her gut.

Swimming alone in the river would have been peaceful under any other circumstances, but she was constantly checking over her shoulder. Though, it did feel refreshing to stretch her wounded fin in the clearer water of the flowing river. The lake was always sort of muddy, and the recent winds had made it more so with the choppy water.

A school of river gar raced along with her for a while as she neared the turn-off where she hoped to find the Grandmerm. Though not as big as the ones that lived in the lake, they were still massive. Soon though, they left her side, taking a branch that she did not follow. She was close, and small signs of a merfolk living in the area began to appear, so she slowed down.

Clumps of shells that were unmistakably harvested, as well as small gardens of edible water plants, were apparent for someone who knew what to look for.

River merfolk were usually solitary. They choose the confines of rivers because they did not want to even occasionally spend time with distant relatives. But everyone needed some connection, so the merfolk in lakes and deltas typically kept track of and checked in with anyone who chose to live alone at least once a year. There was even someone Dani had heard of who lived in a pond in some fancy neighborhood in an old part of Tulsa, but that might have been a rumor.

Merfolk needed quite a lot of space to live, which was why, up until a hundred years or so ago, there were almost no lake merfolk in North America. But after the Dam Lake Act of 1937, more and more lakes were made in places like Oklahoma, so groups of merfolk families began to migrate inland.

The signs of merfolk continued to increase, and Dani knew she was close. She took a deep gulp of water through her gills and stopped swimming before calling out, "Hello? My name is Dani, and I'm looking for Grandmerm Sarnas."

"Which one are you, then?"

As if by magic, a voice came from directly behind Dani so suddenly, she shrieked.

Dani composed herself and elaborated, stating that her home was Lake Hobotnica and giving the names of her parents. She hoped Sarnas would recognize them.

Sarnas gave her an appraising look up and down. "Sorry to have startled you, but you can't be too careful these days."

Dani wasn't sure how scaring the silt out of someone was being careful, but at least the old woman hadn't dismissed or stabbed her.

Sarnas's hair was a deep coal black, braided, and it flowed freely around her head, wild in the flowing river water, like shining snakes coiled around her umber face. She was stunning, and that did not help Dani's nerves. Her clothing looked like armor. It was a vaguely military style, but worn in, coated in a layer of crushed shells.

"I know that I'm intruding, but I need your counsel." Dani bowed her head slightly to show her respect.

"Do you, now?" She swam closer to Dani and circled around her once, quickly. Sarnas pulled around and stopped in front of her, arms crossed. She was not as long as Dani, but she felt much larger.

The part of the river they were in was deep enough that they could float upright, though Dani remained slightly bent in deference.

"I think our people are in great danger." Dani half-expected a gasp of shock from the elder at those words.

But Grandmerm Sarnas just gave a derisive snort.

So, Dani rephrased. "Actually, I know they are. And I need your help."

"Where are your parents?"

"Spawning."

"I truly never saw the point in spawning. Coupling just seems like a waste of energy." Sarnas laughed. "But okay, come with me."

"I am worried the danger might be following me," Dani admitted. She didn't want to bring Muir anywhere he might do more harm.

Sarnas gestured her forward. "We'll be safe where we're going. I've made sure of that."

Sarnas gave her a reassuring nod, and the two of them took off.

They swam a short distance then took a turn off the river a few hundred feet further. Dani sensed a big, human-made structure in the water not too far away, and she wondered what it was. She also sensed some sort of barrier for the first time. It was distinct and comforting, and Dani suddenly realized what Kye had been talking about when they described the protection they felt crossing onto their property.

Sarnas seemed to sense her hesitation and recognition because she, too, paused for a moment then nodded at Dani to keep following and led her to a structure made by the branches and roots of a tree.

The tree grew into the side of the river, half in the earth and half in the water. The roots and branches had been shaped to make a domed room that was much more spacious than Dani first expected. Years of the river's flow had thatched the sides of the structure with caught algae and leaves, but it was clearly cared for and cleared off regularly because there was no damming.

The top of the branches opened up to let sunlight inside, and the effect was enchanting.

Sarnas gestured for Dani to take a seat on several large, smoothed stones, and in moments, the elder had presented Dani with small bowls covered in mesh and filled with tasty, tiny silvery fish snacks. The cage tops kept the small fish from floating away, and they were meaty and salty. Not that she wasn't grateful for the sandwiches and snacks her human friends graciously shared with her meal after meal, but Dani had been eating so much land food the last few days, she relished the freshness of food harvested directly from the river waters.

They ate a few at a time through a small opening in the ceramic bowls. Usually, it took too much patience to scoop up enough of the thin, silver fish to make a snack for oneself, let alone enough to share, so it was even more of a treat.

Dani sensed it was time for her to return the gesture of friendship and pulled out what she hoped was the right choice of offering.

Turned out a six pack of Red Stripe and a bag of beef jerky was, in fact, an extremely adequate offering, and Sarnas clapped in delight.

Sarnas stowed her gifts in an ice chest and gave Dani her full attention. "So, tell me what's going on."

"Have you heard of the Church of the Flood?"

That was all the information Sarnas needed to hear to understand the seriousness of Dani's fears.

"This has happened before," she said solemnly, casting her eyes down.

"What?" Dani asked, startled. "No one ever told us about it."

"It was not a time any of your ancestors would willingly revisit, even if it is at the expense of erasing part of our history," Sarnas explained. "And your parents were too young to remember, if they were even alive."

"When did this happen?" Dani was frustrated for not the first time that there were whole swaths of history she had not been taught. Whether it was human led or merfolk, there were constant moments of revelation when gaps in her education shown through.

At least having her GED might lead her to getting into a college and accessing more history and science. But the purposeful ignorance was infuriating.

Sarnas seemed to wait a beat while Dani had those rapid thoughts.

"Before our people's migration to the lakes and rivers," the elder said at last, "there was much infighting as the brackish swamp lands and bogs became more and more overcrowded with humans."

"That's what is happening here too," Dani said. Over the past few years, the lake had dramatically increased in human population and boat traffic.

"While they may appear to be trying to help the environment, the Church of the Flood has one goal and that is destruction. Focusing on infrastructure that is there to block the waters and shape the lands."

"One of our own, Muir, is involved." Dani said, and Sarnas nodded. "He's helping this cult. Said he's part of a bigger thing."

"Yes, The Church of the Flood has followed our people for generations, harnessing the powers of the merfolk to bring about their destructive plans. And they anticipated our arrival, establishing a presence before the dams were even built. They seek those powerful enough to open the portals which lead to terrible destruction. Though few are powerful enough to control them once they are brought forth."

"Kinda makes you miss good old-fashioned evangelism." Dani said.

Sarnas broke her sagely elder vibes for a second and snorted. "You have no idea."

"But you can help us stop it?" Dani asked earnestly. "And can you help me keep the school safe?"

"I will help you any way that I can." Sarnas put their bowls away, grabbed a small bag, and double checked the latch on the cooler. "But right now, we must swim while we talk. I have something you have to see."

Dani nodded, and the two of them swam from the underwater home upriver.

The older merfolk swam with agility that Dani envied. Lake life, where there was ample space and relatively still waters, had made her passive in her swimming. She had been upriver only a handful of times but had heard of the power and strength required to navigate oceans and deltas. Her life in the mostly calm lake waters was cushy, and the way

Sarnas twisted and turned made Dani wish she'd spent more time in rougher seas.

She watched how the older merfolk worked her way around rocks and through shallow parts and tree roots without having to stop or slow, and Dani worked to mimic her techniques, soon keeping up.

"When this has happened before, it took cooperation with human allies to stop it." The Grandmerm spoke to her as they swam. "The Church of the Flood has led its followers and our people to this destruction before, and they will try again. It is a cycle, but we can stop it."

"You've done it before?"

"Yes, long ago. They're constantly trying to flood the whole earth. But now it's up to the younger generation."

"Well, that sounds like a big ask." Dani was not in the mood to take on a quest. She was tired and kinda just wanted to bring her the kids to Sarnas and take a nap and maybe this old lady would take care of everything for her. Plus, her tail still ached, though it was healing up nicely.

"I'm far too old to wield magical weapons and battle demons," Sarnas added as if reading Dani's thoughts. "But I will arm you with the tools of your ancestors."

They took one last turn, and the large structure that Dani had sensed came into view below the water.

"Is that a submarine?" She had never seen one in person before now, because even living one's whole life in water, when in the world was that supposed to come up? "How in the redneck heck did it get to Oklahoma?"

"That's a story for another time, but let's just say gumption." Sarnas unwrapped a cloth from around her forearm. It was black and had white stitching on it. She found a piece of wood and tied the cloth around it.

"What are you doing?"

"I'm letting our human allies know that we are once again working together."

"Wait, you know humans?"

Sarnas nodded. "I'm guessing you do as well."

Dani said nothing but nodded.

"Good." Sarnas gave a small smile and put her arm on Dani's. "This next part doesn't work if you don't have land-walking allies. Are these humans you trust?"

An image of Kye and Florence laughing together on the pier while they skipped stones flashed through her head, followed by an image of Kye as Dani faded into and out of consciousness. Never afraid because Kye's face kept being there every time she started to wake up.

"Yes. Yes, I trust them."

"Good. Because there are some things they'll need to do."

Chapter 11 Kye

"Well, this just gets weirder and weirder." Kye and Florence were flipping through the scrapbook Kye had taken from Muir's trunk, and it was one of the strangest things either of them had ever seen. Muir had obviously been sneaking around with the cult for ages, based on the span of photographs. Many of them were Polaroids taken on land during church activities such as a particularly unsettling one of him at a church picnic potluck.

Growing up, they had always been so careful to not take photos of themselves with the merfolk and vice versa because secrecy was so important and they didn't want to get caught.

It was jarring seeing Muir just laid out on a picnic blanket holding a plate of potato salad, grilled chicken, and deviled eggs, posing with half a dozen church ladies.

"How did he manage to get away with this?" Florence pointed to a photo of him at a pageant of some sort. "Who is he dressed as?"

Kye peered closer. "Maybe a shepherd? It's hard to tell."

"This is just wild." Florence shook her head. "I almost don't want to look anymore."

"Yeah, but it's hard to turn away." Kye took the book when she handed it to them and thumbed through a few more pages. "I'm not sure how he pulled it off, but Dani got her GED in secret, so maybe their folks just don't pay as much attention as ours would?"

For every scrapbook photo collage, there was another page of rantings and writings that sounded biblical but were clearly cult specific. They came to a photo of some younger people, and Kye pointed at one.

"I think I saw this one at the gas station yesterday," Kye said. "How many times have we bumped into them and not known how deep this went?"

"Let me talk to him," Florence said softly.

"Un-freaking-likely." Kye looked at her like she had mustard on her face.

"He and I have a history. Maybe I could reason with him."

"When I saw him yesterday, it was like Muir on steroids but not just the kind for when your allergies are bad. The kind all those baseball players used in the nineties," Kye said. "He has plans he's set on, and he really doesn't want us to interfere."

"Well, me talking to him shouldn't hurt then." Florence crossed her arms, and Kye groaned internally at their stubborn friend. "If he's going through with it, he's going through with it, and he knows I won't be able to stop him anyway."

"I'm not going to let you put yourself into physical danger." Kye took her by both shoulders and looked her in the eyes. "You're far too lovely to risk."

She laughed then shook her head. "We have to at least try. Our best bet is going to be stopping whatever the cult is trying to do before it happens, right?"

"Well, I'm not just sending you to get kidnapped and held for ransom. Or worse, you get turned over to the dark side and become part of the cult yourself."

"I just think, if we can talk to him, reason with him, we might be able to get through." Florence wrapped her arms around herself, looking sad. "He wasn't always such a douche canoe."

Kye laughed. "Well, that's true. Though he's always been at least a little bit of one."

She couldn't disagree. "Too bad he doesn't have a cell phone."

"Hey, that gives me an idea."

There was no way Kye was going to feel safe with Florence talking to Muir one on one. They may

81

have been closer than any of the others at times, and Florence may have had a thing for him for a few middle school years, but Kye was not in the habit of putting their best friend's life in danger.

And Muir was nothing if not a danger.

They came up with a compromise, and Florence had put out whatever secret signal she and Muir had used when they were around thirteen so they could meet up.

But instead of face to face, Muir was met with a high-range walkie-talkie. Yes, Kye's parents would be livid with them if one got lost, but it was the best way they could figure to let Florence talk to him.

From their vantage point on the tailgate of Florence's truck and using their parents' binocular set, Kye saw Muir shake his head and grab the walkie-talkie. For a second, Kye thought he might just throw the radio into the lake and swim away, but they could hear what sounded like amusement in his voice when he spoke to Florence, who was standing a few yards away with her own binoculars.

Kye wanted to give her a bit of privacy but also wanted to make sure that whatever Muir had to say didn't in any way make Florence doubt herself. Sometimes her anxiety put her in emotional guilt loops and Kye was wary about putting her in the situation to begin with.

"I don't know what you hope to accomplish with this conversation, Florence," Muir said it with a smirk and a small wave in their direction.

He had easily spotted the truck.

"Hey to you too, Muir." Florence shifted on her feet when, for a few beats, he didn't reply. "Seriously, Muir, talk to me. Please."

"I'm not sure what it is you're wanting to talk about, Florence." He was resting in the shallows nonchalantly like he had all the time in the world and there wasn't about to be a huge freaking reckoning.

"We're worried about you and about whatever it is that's happening." Florence was always looking for the best in people, no matter how long it had been since they were close. It had been ages since Muir and Florence had been involved, and over the past couple of summers, they'd all drifted apart. But there was something about that first crush, and Florence was never one to walk away from a friend. "We want to try and keep you safe."

"You keep saying 'we' like we're still kids. Our paths diverged a lot more than y'all like to think. It's all nostalgia for you. I'm here to affect the future."

"How do you plan on doing that?" She was trying to get him to give her more information about the plans. If they could stop whatever it was before it happened, everything would be easier. If only they'd seen signs that Muir was acting strangely, they might have seen this coming years ago.

"I have some very powerful allies. The Church of the Flood sees my power and my potential, and our values align." He sounded like he was just regurgitating lines that had been fed to him.

Some Kye recognized from the scrapbook rantings. Kye was ready to cut things short, certain that they'd get nowhere, but Florence waved them off.

"You know it's a cult, right?" Florence's scolding tone was certainly transmitted through the walkie-talkie. "Muir, they're so off the wall. And they always have been. They're into some deep stuff." She threw her hands in the air as she said it.

There was another pause, though Kye wasn't confident that Muir was actually thinking things through. "Don't be so quick to judge."

Florence huffed, blowing her bangs out of her eyes. Kye had been on the receiving end of that huff and was not keen to repeat it.

Sure enough, she brought out the big guns.

"Does your momma know you've been talking to them?" she asked.

His mom was a fairly hardcore church lady. Florence had never been certain which denomination they belonged to, but it was definitely not like the Church of the Flood, which was mostly hellfire and brimstone and super into the Jonah and the whale story, based on what they'd gleaned from the pamphlets and—Kye shuddered at the thought—Muir's scrapbook.

"My momma doesn't get to dictate my faith," Muir said.

Florence groaned, but not on the radio.

"Ask him how he got in with them," Kye suggested. If he wasn't even worried about his mom, he was further gone than any of them might have guessed.

She nodded.

"So, how'd you get signed up for this? They go fishing for a merfolk, and you took the bait?" She was being sassier than usual, and Kye liked it.

"Yes, they sought me out." He sounded proud. Like he had when Kye had approached him on the dock with the cultists. "I was prophesied."

"You were prophesied?" Florence tried her best to keep her voice neutral. But the look she gave Kye let them know they were in agreement. This was bad.

"Once in a century, a merfolk is born with the powers to harness the creature brought forth by the Church of the Flood. With that power, I will reshape our lands."

Florence looked at Kye with wide eyes and mouthed, creature?

"Ask what kind of creature," Kye whispered, even though Florence had her finger off the radio.

"What kind of creature?" She seemed determined to get some information from Muir that wasn't just confirmation of his exploding bravado.

"One of unspeakable powers and might. One that will churn the waters and tear down what is wrongfully built."

Kye was scribbling quickly in their notebook, assuming that everything Muir was spouting off was straight from the Flood Cult Handbook. As he spoke, the waters around him seemed to bubble and rock, and Kye swore the clouds got darker.

From the spot where he napped in the back of the truck, Bruno opened one eye then, glancing at Kye, seemed to see that they were paying attention and closed it again.

"We want to help you, Muir." Florence pleaded with him one last time.

He scoffed at her. "You help me? I'm about to be the most powerful merfolk to ever set fin in these waters."

"It's just a lake in Oklahoma."

"That's where we begin. But not where we end."

"Where will it end?"

There was the longest pause yet.

"I have no reason to speak with you anymore. Goodbye," Muir said.

"Wait!" she shouted back into the radio. "Aren't you worried about your family? Your neighbors?"

They could see he wasn't swimming away, but it was hard to tell if he had put down the walkie-talkie or not.

"Dani's out there upriver trying to find help for the school, and you don't even care what happens to any of them." Florence slapped a hand over her mouth as soon as the words came out.

There was a pregnant pause on the channel.

"So, Dani isn't home anymore." His voice crackled over the radio, and he was swimming away. "I'll send her your regards."

Then the radio cut to static.

"Oh silt, Kye."

"She'll be okay." Kye wasn't going to let themself worry. There was nothing they could do. They needed to get home. Dani should be back soon.

Florence and Kye jumped back in the truck.

Chapter 12 Dani

An hour later, Dani had a couple daggers, the start of a plan, and a long list of instructions for Kye and Florence, as well as herself and Billy. Sarnas had shown her so much, and while Dani had wanted to stick around and pick her brain, they both knew time was running out if there was going to be any hope of stopping Muir and the Church of the Flood and getting the school to safety.

"Stay safe and swim fast." Sarnas helped Dani tuck the daggers away safely and continued to give instructions after they had left the USS Stonefish. "How many are in the school?"

"Fourteen including me and Billy." Dani was studying the maps that Sarnas had shown her, hoping to memorize them.

"It'll be better if they're just in your head. We don't want the cult to find these locations any sooner than they probably will on their own. You'll want to make sure the school comes with any supplies they might need for the next couple of days as well."

Dani nodded. "I already have their medications gathered up. Billy will help me with the rest."

"Good." Sarnas looked her over and put her hands on Dani's shoulders. "Now hurry back. If things have progressed as quickly as you describe, we are running out of time to keep the school safe."

"Stay safe. Swim fast," Dani repeated to Sarnas, and after a quick hug that made Dani miss her folks, she left.

Dani hurried back the way she'd come, hoping to reach the lake house in plenty of time to both prepare Billy and the younger kids, as well as Kye and Florence for what they needed to do.

She was so focused on the tasks ahead, that she was barely paying attention to her surroundings, so the sudden appearance of Muir at the mouth of the river took her by surprise.

"Muir." She pulled up short, her way blocked by his tattooed body. There were some definite downsides to being in a narrow river versus the openness of the lake.

"Dani." He crossed his bulging arms across his chest. The tattoos on his torso glowed softly in the slanted afternoon light.

"Right, so I'm just gonna head on back home now." She didn't want him to see her shake, and she sure as heck wanted to get out of there and to the safety of the wards.

Sarnas had explained to her that several of the areas around the lake had been warded by her or her human contact to keep certain places safe. But the spot where Dani swam now, within ten feet of Muir, was not one of those protected spaces.

"What are you doing here?" he asked, looking past her suspiciously.

"Just out for a swim." She moved a fraction of a wave to the right.

He mirrored her movement, clear in his intention to block her way until he got the information he wanted.

"In the river?" He was clearly suspicious, and Dani was kicking herself for not paying closer attention. She could have even had Kye pick her up upriver or something.

"It's not really any of your business, is it." She tried changing tactics and laid on the annoyed friend tone. "Not after what you've done."

He had the audacity to roll his eyes at her.

"Just let me pass, Muir, I don't have anything to say to you."

He squinted his eyes at her but didn't move. She made to swim past him and for a moment, thought that he'd let her.

But at the last second, he grabbed her bag and ripped it off her shoulder.

"Hey, what the heck, Muir." She yelped, swimming toward him with her arm out. "Give that back."

She made to grab the bag, but he held it away from her.

"I think I'll keep it since you're failing to be forthcoming about your reason for being in this river."

She reached for it one more time then, in a huff, pushed her way past him and swam away as quickly as she could. Muir could keep her bag full of his own Church of the Flood fliers and the two empty bottles of Red Stripe.

As Dani swam to the dock and made her way safely across the wards, she patted her vest, feeling for the daggers Sarnas had gifted her which remained tucked safely against her chest.

Florence and Kye were waiting for her on the dock. Florence was clearly in tears, and Kye's face was in a tight grimace. They both gasped, and Florence let out an "ohthankyoujesus" when Dani hopped onto the dock in one piece.

"Dani, I'm so sorry, I accidentally told Muir where you were." Florence full-on sobbed.

"Hey, I'm okay." Dani pulled her friend into a hug. "Now, could you please go make us some tea. I have about a thousand things to tell you all."

Florence wiped away a few tears and then went up to the house to put on the kettle.

Dani let out a breath she was holding. "So that was really scary."

She shook as Kye reached out and pulled her into a tight hug.

"I'm so sorry we told Muir where you were," Kye murmured, holding Dani close and rubbing her back.

Dani shook her head. "He would have found me. He's on the hunt. I think the church need more merfolk for what they're doing. We've been safe because of some wards."

Kye didn't seem surprised and just nodded. "I figured something like that was protecting us. I feel it stronger and stronger now that I know what I'm feeling for."

"There is so much we have to do." Dani didn't want to cry. It was too early for that. She took a deep breath and let herself relax into Kye's arms. "Okay. I'm okay."

But Kye didn't let go right away and hugged her even more tightly. Then Dani felt Kye stiffen.

Kye pulled back and looked at her curiously. "Are you wearing, knives?"

"Oh yeah, check it out." Dani was glad for the change of subject because for a moment she thought that maybe she could just stay with Kye on the dock for a few days and ignore all the rest of the world. She reached behind her and unhooked her vest to pull out the two daggers that Sarnas had gifted her.

"Whoa." Kye's eyes widened eagerly when Dani handed them the pair.

They were obviously a set, though one was about six inches shorter than the other. Both were thin and a bit flexible like a fish boning knife but with hooked ends, making them more versatile.

"Sarnas seemed to think they would come in handy," Dani said with a shudder. She was happy to defend herself from Muir, but the thought of using something like the daggers gave her the heebie-jeebies.

Kye, on the other hand, seemed to take to them immediately.

"These have a nice weight to them." Kye held one in each hand, balancing them first on the flat edge then holding the handles. The blades had several runes carved into them along the blades and looked ancient. But the handles were quite modern.

"Sarnas said she got tired of the old handles and upgraded to a heavy-duty rubber set a few decades ago. She said it's the same stuff they made boar grips out of, though I do not know what that means."

"It's for hunting boar with a handgun. You gotta use really big bullets." Kye laughed. "No idea where that info popped up from."

"Well, keep it filed away for 'how to kill monsters' trivia night." Dani took the daggers back and tucked them into her vest. "I'm really glad Muir didn't take them. Though I really liked that bag."

"Okay, what did I miss?" Florence reappeared with a tray full of tea and all the stuff to make s'mores. They both looked at her, and she shrugged. "I figure you have a lot to fill us in on, and we do too, and I'm not gonna let these marshmallows go to waste."

The other two started to protest.

But Florence held up a hand. "We all need sleep, and it's too late to do anything tonight. So come on. It's campfire time."

Dani hadn't realized how tense she was until she took a sip of the tea Florence handed her and a spot by the fire pit. They'd chosen to set up on the small, rocky beach rather than up at the dock so Dani could get to the water easier. Kye made quick work getting the fire going, and the warmth was welcome in the chilly evening air. Dani would never completely get used to the sudden changes in temperature the air imposed, but she loved the crisp heat that came from campfires.

"So, we have a lot to talk about." Dani took the bag of marshmallows from Florence and began to fill them in on her visit to Sarnas.

"We didn't really accomplish much." Florence looked down and poked the fire with a stick. "Just gave away your location and ticked off Muir."

"Hey, don't beat yourself up." Dani reached over and gave Florence's hand a squeeze. "One of us would have tried to talk to him at some point. We owed that to ourselves to try."

"And now we can go thwart all of Muir's evil plans guilt free." Kye pointed out with finger guns. "By the way, can I hold the magic daggers again?"

Dani laughed. "Sarnas didn't say they were magic."

"Obviously they're magic." Kye's eyes gleamed as they took the daggers from Dani, holding them to the firelight. "So, what do we need to do?"

Dani spent the next hour going over the plans, wishing they had more time. And between the three of them, they killed the whole bag of marshmallows.

Chapter 13 Kye

First thing the next morning, Kye and Florence loaded up in the truck and headed to the USS Stonefish.

Though they spotted him right away, the docent was showing around a couple that obviously belonged to the RV parked out front based on their cargo shorts and Route 66 T-shirts. Despite their urgency, they wanted to wait until the guide was alone before approaching him.

"Let's go look around." If it had been under any other circumstance, Kye would have been super eager to explore, so they decided they may as well check out the museum while they waited.

The first section was just a small set of rooms with glass cases holding items from several wars.

But the outside was where it really outshone itself as a unique museum.

Walking down a stone path and onto a ramp, they made their way across the metal bridge that connected the submarine to the land. As they went, they passed several other decommissioned vehicles and giant weapons.

Kye gaped at the submarine. "I can't believe I've never been here before."

"Wait till you see inside," Florence said, excited to climb back down into the musty metal.

On the drive, she'd told Kye all about visiting it with her dad years ago, but seeing it in person was something else. Florence said she'd spent plenty of time daydreaming about what she would do if she were traveling on one, and Kye could totally see why.

They climbed in but didn't linger, though it was tempting. All of the buttons and levers and doors still opened and moved and closed, but there just wasn't any power except going to the lights and fans at either end. It probably turned into an oven during the summer months, but for now, the temperature was pleasant.

It was impossible to not touch stuff, and as they made their way from one hatch section to another, there were very few levers left un-pulled.

When they got to the far end of the submarine and climbed back up into the sun, the brightness made them both squint after the dim lighting inside. Florence rattled off some facts about pirate eye patches, and they couldn't help indulging themselves by taking a few selfies next to the big gun on the bow.

Half an hour later, they wandered back into the museum and looked around until the couple with the RV waved goodbye and exited to the parking lot.

"Is that you, sir?" Florence asked, pointing at a photograph on the wall that was taken on the deck of the USS Stonefish.

His grin widened from one of kindness to one of pride. "Yes, miss, it is. Richard Harold."

"You served on the USS Stonefish, Mr. Harold?" Kye peered at the photograph as well.

"Yes, I did. And y'all can call me Richard. Mr. Harold was my father," he said in a way that assured both of them he'd been repeating the same joke for forty years, minimum.

"Nice to meet you." Kye reached out their hand and shook his. "I'm Kye, they/them."

"And I'm Florence, she/her." Florence took his hand next.

"Pleased to meet you both," Mr. Harold smiled at them.

Kye was suddenly nervous but asked anyway. "You happen to know a Sarnas?"

It seemed to Kye that Mr. Harold got really still. Then he took in a breath, "I thought she might be sending y'all when I saw her signal."

Florence and Kye nodded.

"Well then, we probably have lots to talk about." He walked over to the door and flipped the sign from open to closed.

"Are you sure it's okay to close this early?" Kye asked as he locked the door.

"It's Muskogee on a weekday, it's sorta chilly, and there aren't any school trips. It'll be fine." He gave a small chuckle. "Y'all can go sit down in the conference room. I'll lock up the back and be right in."

Kye and Florence made their way to the back room, which was jam-packed with bookshelves and filing cabinets floor to ceiling. In the center of the room was a round, solid wood table and six chairs that looked straight out of the seventies. When Mr. Harold came in, he walked purposefully over to a filing cabinet to the right of a storage closet, and from the middle of a pile of what looked like old tax receipts, he pulled a lock box.

"Have a seat, friend." He gestured to Kye, who was still standing, peering at the shelves along the walls full of old books and model ships and framed medals. "Before I can show you anything in this box, I need to ask you a few questions."

They both nodded solemnly.

"And," he continued, "I need you to answer them honestly because many lives may be at stake."

"We will," Kye said.

"Are you members of the Church of the Flood?" he asked, and they both started.

"No," they answered in a chorus of denial, trying not to be overly zealous about their disdain for the cult.

"Are you?" Florence asked back, and he shook his head.

"Is that like how cops are supposed to say they're cops?" Kye wondered aloud.

"Mostly, it's just to get a feel for who Sarnas has sent me and to find out how much you know and how much more you need to know," Mr. Harold said. Kye might have been imagining it, but the way he said Sarnas sounded reverent, if not wistful.

"Basically, we know that there's a cult trying to tear down the dam and somehow they got one of the merfolk to work with them, and we need directions on how to stop it." Kye spoke quickly, hoping that they were covering the basics enough to get going.

"Oh, right. Yeah, that's..." Mr. Harold said. "That's pretty much it."

"If you could give us any other information about how to fight this, we would be so grateful." Florence leaned forward on her elbows, eager to pick his brain.

"There is a lot you all do not know." He opened the box and took a few items out of it. Most seemed to be newspaper clippings, and he pushed them over to Kye and Florence.

The one Kye got was a deployment announcement for the USS Stonefish during a war. They traced their fingers across the black-and-white image and found Richard right away.

Another was a clipping about the astounding return of the USS Stonefish after the Navy had assumed it had been sunk.

Florence's was one about the crew coming to a fifty-year celebration of the decommissioning of their submarine.

"During the war we saw many things," Mr. Harold said, "but none were quite so fear-inducing as the creatures summoned from the deep that first time."

"Wait, creatures?" Kye grimaced. "Plural?"

"The first time?" Florence interjected.

Mr. Harold nodded gravely, taking his worn baseball cap off and setting it on the table next to the box. "Though some were smaller potatoes than others."

"It was the cult then too?" Kye asked, looking over the clippings.

"It's always a cult," Florence said with a sad sigh.

"The enemy helped us. We were in the ocean, and while out on a routine patrol, we encountered our first of the demons completely unexpectedly. It almost sank us, but our captain was quite clever, and we made it out relatively intact. We were separated from our fleet and two smaller enemy vessels from

101

theirs. Once we realized we had all been thrown far from the sea fights and well out of range of any other radio signals, we began communicating with each other, trying to figure out just what in the heck was happening.

"One of the smaller ships was taking on water, and we had room. All of us on both sides were hesitant at first, but once we admitted to one another what we had seen, we decided to work together to figure out what we had to do to stop those creatures from devouring the rest of our fleets."

"So how did you stop it?" Kye asked.

"Partly, it was luck." He flipped through the items that remained in the box. "Partly, it was cooperation. And also, a lot of it was desperation."

Mr. Harold slid a photo across to the middle of the table where they could both see it.

A harpoon gun almost identical to the one that they had seen on top of the USS Stonefish, minus all the paint and extra bolts to keep school kids from knocking it off and smashing themselves, was featured prominently in the photo, along with two sailors, leaning against the barrel.

"The only reason we escaped from that first attack," Mr. Harold said, "was that we were on the surface when it began. The demon sank half a dozen other vessels that day. It was just pure luck that we had the means to fight it off the next time."

"Why did you have the harpoon gun?" Kye asked, eyeing the photograph.

"Part of the cooperation was with the merfolk. Including my friend Sarnas, who it seems we know through a mutual friend. They were on both sides, just like the humans, and the right ones found us in time to use the weapon."

"Wow, that does sound unbelievably lucky," Kye was impressed.

"Just wait until you hear about how lucky we got when we actually shot the thing. Only needed one of the three harpoons," he said smugly.

"Right, well, let's hope we have the same amount of luck," Florence said. "Can you show us where the gun is and help us figure out how to use it?"

"Sure, it's safe at my house, hidden behind some enchantments that very few could hope to break through even if they knew how," he said. "The cultists aren't the only ones with spells."

Tucking the illustrations and newspaper clippings carefully back into the file box, he stood.

"We appreciate any help you can give us and you taking the time to tell us your story." Kye nodded at him.

"Of course," Mr. Harold said. "I don't get to tell a lot of folks about what happened out there."

"I imagine not. They'd think you'd lost it completely," Florence added.

"Yeah, add that to being old and trying to explain to folks you work on a submarine in Oklahoma. You've got the perfect combination to not be taken seriously." He chuckled.

"Well, we believe you and appreciate your commitment to helping us and the area again." Florence reached over and gave his hand a squeeze.

"First, you'll need to get the harpoons for it," Mr. Harold said. "I'd rather not take down my wards until you have those."

"Where do we find them?" Kye asked.

"I can tell you right where they are," he told them, "but after that, I don't want to know what you do with the information. Plausible deniability has kept many of my secrets safe."

"Understood." Kye nodded.

"The Church of the Flood has interests in more than just the dam, and much of their power comes from the earth in the form of oil," Mr. Harold explained. "It's kept them in money and power for years in Oklahoma, and it's why they were set up here well before the dams."

Kye and Florence nodded.

"Are y'all familiar with The Ranhills Estate?"

"Yes, we are." Kye and Florence had been there a handful of times both with their schools and with their families.

It looked like they were about to check another box on third-grade Oklahoma field-trip bingo.

Chapter 14 Dani

When Kye and Florence left to go meet up with Sarnas's friend, Dani took off as well to collect any supplies she and the school might need over the next couple of days. She wasn't the only one with a pet, and she knew that the kids would be running out of clothes and other supplies. So, she traveled as cautiously as she could, knowing that Muir might be around any corner.

The distance she covered was immense, since most of the families lived far from one another, but she was well rested from the night before and able to swim back at nearly her full speed now that she was mostly healed and in open waters.

Making several stops, she checked her surroundings before entering the space of each family's dwelling. There were several catfish to make sure had food within reach of their thin vine leashes. As well as two alligator snapping turtle twins that belonged to one of the youngsters, Gracie, and which freaked Dani out every time. There were legends that if an alligator snapping turtle bit your finger, it wouldn't let go until lightning struck.

Dani did not enjoy tossing them the few fish she'd caught on the way but managed to do it from a distance and called it good, not bothering to watch as they gobbled them up.

Each home she stopped at, she searched quickly for any food stored that was set aside for the youngsters during the time their parents were gone and added it to the mesh bags she had slung over her shoulder. She didn't enjoy having to drag so much around, but Sarnas had suggested stocking up if there were any supplies on hand, so that's what she was doing.

They'd be leaving as soon as she got back, and she'd be able to distribute the bags to some of the older kiddos.

Dani was almost done and ready to head back to the land house when she heard the distinct sound of a boat motor. Most of the lake had been quiet. The winds were high, and the water was choppier than most folks liked to get out in, not to mention it was the middle of the week in early springtime.

She paused and looked up to see if she could spot the boat. When she did, it was directly above her.

And they were dropping a net.

Dani dove. But they had taken her by surprise, and the net fell unnaturally quickly. In seconds, she was tangled in thick, nylon ropes and being pulled to the surface.

"Not today, turds." She quickly pulled the dagger from her vest and began slicing at the netting.

At first, it did nothing.

The ropes were too thick or protected by some magic, and she couldn't break through.

She tried again and again and only succeeded in slicing part of her finger. Dani let out a hiss at the sting and almost lost her grip on the dagger, but she caught it just in time.

Pulling a *Finding Nemo*, she swam down against the pull of the net and continued to slice with the dagger. Finally, as the light of the surface was closing in, she broke free into the lake waters and swam full speed down and at an angle away from the boat in the opposite direction of the lake home and the school.

But the sound of the boat continued to follow her.

"How are they doing this?" She changed direction and pushed herself to speed up, but it didn't help. The boat turned when she did, again and again.

Finally, she was fed up with being chased and swam until she was on the surface directly in front of the boat, which slowed to a stop. There were half a dozen cultists on the deck staring her down menacingly.

"What do y'all want?" Dani shouted.

"To harness the power of the merfolk and bring about the greatest flood—"

Dani cut off the shouting cultist with a wave. "Yes, yes, I know all that. But why?"

"To bring about a cleansed earth. One where the merfolk have free rein."

"I'm gonna stop you right there." Dani held up a hand. "First of all, none of us wants to live in nasty water that has, like, city trash and sewage and everything else in it. Secondly, I'm really busy and do not have time to keep running from you."

At that, she dove under the water and quickly swam under the boat where she wedged a piece of scrap metal she'd found into the propeller. It wouldn't stop them forever, but it would slow them down. She spotted a Fishfinder mounted on the boat, which explained how they were tracking her and also where a bunch of their church bake-sale fundraising had gone.

Dani dove as deep as she could before swimming in the direction of the lake house, hoping it would take them long enough to fix their motor that she could make it back.

It creeped her out to think about how much they might have been tracking them. Most fishers just chalked up the large size of the merfolk to alligator gar, but if someone knew what to look for, they might have been watching their movements for ages.

If nothing else, it re-emphasized her desire to get the school to safety. For the first time in her life, the lake felt sinister. Like there were enemies around any corner, eyes always watching.

Chapter 15 Kye

"Can we stop by Sonic on our way?" Kye leaned forward from the window seat of Florence's pickup. Kye loved riding in the truck with her, and it was easy to daydream this was just a regular day cruising around finding nothing to do.

Plus, they were already on the way past the Sonic, so there wasn't really a reason not to swing by.

"Yeah, sure thing." She steered the truck along the narrow winding roads that led away from the lake houses and turned it toward town and the highway that would take them to the museum where Mr. Harold had told them the harpoons would be, which they'd confirmed on the museum's website.

The plan was to get the harpoons somehow.

That was it.

That was the whole plan.

Then they'd meet back up with Mr. Harold in the evening.

Hopefully with the harpoons that they would get somehow.

The two of them rode in silence until Florence pulled into the stall, and they looked at the menu, even though they could probably recite the whole thing from memory.

"What do you want?" she asked.

"I'll take a cherry limeade," Kye said. "And a small mozzarella sticks with Ranch."

"Oh, yeah, that sounds good. I'll take some too."

"You got a coupon? Because this is gonna add up fast." Kye handed her their debit card with a joking look.

"Hey, we've been living off sandwiches and s'mores. Not my fault Sonic is gonna hit the spot." Florence shrugged.

"Ooo, are they doing all day breakfast?"

"Oh my gawd." Florence laughed and pushed the red button. She swiped the card for payment after giving the order.

"It's not even happy hour," Kye grumbled under their breath as they heard the total.

A few minutes later, their carhop was skating out with their order. They took a few minutes to get settled, then Florence put the truck into gear, and they got on the road.

The drive to The Ranhills Estate took about an hour and a half, and it was pleasantly warm. Kye hadn't gotten to spend much time with Florence over the last year since they were both seniors and had a lot of things on their plates. Florence especially was involved in pretty much every other extracurricular activity. Kye's school was significantly smaller, but there was still always something to do.

Kye was about to ask her how the prom planning was going since she had been on the committee the previous year, but before they could, Florence was already back on the subject of heisting.

"I think it will be easier to steal if there are lots of people around," she said.

"How do you figure?" Kye asked.

"If we have more people milling around, we're more able to be ambiguous about who it is who took it, and it provides opportunities for cover."

"That makes sense, I suppose," Kye said thoughtfully.

"Ooo! And we can use my family's museum pass." She had jumped directly from a great idea to a not great one, but Kye loved the enthusiasm.

"I mean, do you want the cops to call your folks when you're under investigation for stealing some of their stuff?" Kye pointed out.

Florence deflated. "Oh, right."

"So, anyway, we'll be using cash." Kye laughed. "That's like Be Gay Do Crime 101. Don't worry. You'll catch on."

"I honestly think I'm gonna be way better at the criminal stuff than you are." Florence put on her sunglasses and rolled down her truck window, sticking an arm out with a wink.

"All right, Clyde, calm down." Kye laughed and rolled down their own window.

On the way to the museum, Kye tried to not focus too hard on having to steal a set of magical harpoons from one of the largest oil baron family legacy museums in the country. At least not so hard they would get to the point of asking Florence to pull a U-turn.

"Maybe we just focus on how ridiculous it is that they have them to begin with. I feel like being angry is better than nervous." Florence took a bite of her burrito, the smell of sausage and cheese product making Kye regret every decision they'd made that didn't end up with ordering one themself. She must have noticed them drooling because she motioned toward them with the burrito. "Want a bite?"

"Nah, I'm good," Kye said because they had enough pride to not take a bite from Florence's almost completely devoured breakfast. This was on them. This complete lapse in judgment. They'd have to live with the consequences. They took another bite of mozzarella stick.

"I think you're right." Kye took a drink and rolled the window down a little more so they could rest their arm outside. "If you think about it, that museum is definitely on the worse side of museum collections."

"I haven't been there since a sixth grade field trip," Florence said. "All I remember is the giant airplane?"

"Probably because you blocked out the hundreds of taxidermied animals."

"Eww, really?" she shuddered.

"Yeah, you are not going to enjoy it." Kye wasn't looking forward to seeing how she reacted to the displays. It wasn't going to be pretty.

"Well, at least it's not like they're keeping live animals captive. And I might take it upon myself to snatch a few extra things on our way out to re-appropriate them for good measure." Florence reached over and turned on the radio, scanning until Kye grabbed her hand.

"Wait, this one," they said.

"Merle Haggard?" Florence gave Kye a quick side eye.

"What? It's catchy."

"Okay, weirdo."

The museum grounds were exactly like Kye had remembered them, and it was both nostalgic and eerie.

The two of them smiled but, like, in a normal and not at all totally suspicious way, at the docent in the small entrance building who took their cash and handed them two tickets, a parking slip to put on the dashboard of the truck, and two copies of the map,

115

which included the handful of separate buildings on one side and the different exhibits in the main museum on the other.

Kye nodded when Florence looked pointedly at the markings along the arch that stretched over the road at the entrance. They seemed innocuous but matched the patterns Muir had tattooed on his chest, the arches around the Church of the Flood, and the ones Kye had seen peeking out from the dam authority dude's sleeves.

"Should we have packed, like, ski masks?" Florence asked after they had pulled away from the ticket gate.

"If we were going to wear ski masks, we would have needed to bring a grappling hook too." Kye said. "Gone in *Mission Impossible* style."

"I packed my pepper spray." She shrugged slightly.

"Okay, but that's not the same as like doing a movie bank heist. That's just common sense," Kye said. "And you always have your pepper spray."

"I still think maybe we should have done more to, like, hide our appearances or disguise ourselves." She glanced at her reflection in the rearview mirror then over at Kye.

"If this works," Kye continued, "it'll be way better for us in the short term if we just look like any other group of visitors. Anything else might get us caught much faster. So, for now, we're just two pals, looking at the well-preserved legacy of a racist dead white man for a fun afternoon outing."

"I can't believe Dani gets to go meet elder merfolk mystics and we're stuck on racist oil dude duty."

They looked around as Florence drove down the winding, hilly road. The museum had one big, circular driveway that led in and out of the land that was all part of the estate. On the way to the main grounds, they passed such a bizarre collection of random animals that both of them kept having to do double takes.

"Do you think they hunt those animals?" Florence asked with a grimace.

"Um, I definitely wouldn't be surprised," Kye said, not at all excited about showing their best friend, who got squeamish at roadkill while driving past it at seventy-five miles per hour, the menagerie of taxidermied heads that awaited them both

"I swear to god, rich white men are the absolute freaking worst." She shook her head.

"Yup," Kye agreed.

Both of them knew that they would feel less than zero guilt about stealing from this rich dude's money pile. They'd been doing more research on their hour-long drive in-between dead zones, and it wasn't a good look. Lots of "acquired" art and artifacts—a.k.a., ripping off Indigenous people and making the white oil people a pretty little place to visit on the weekends. Museum acquisitions were just one of the many ways white people collect other cultures.

There was worse than the taxidermied animal collection at the museum, and after going there on so many field trips, Kye was surprised more of their classmates hadn't turned out to be environmental activists.

"We're almost there." Florence pulled into the half-filled parking lot.

"I'm surprised it's so busy on a weekday," Kye said as they found a parking spot near the Lodge.

"Give me a second. I have to back in."

"What do you mean?"

"I mean, 'shush' so I can focus." She shot them a look.

"Can I get out? Apparently, you're really bad at parking. I don't want to be injured."

Florence slammed on the brakes and glared. "I am *not* bad at parking. I just don't like backing in to park."

"Right, sorry." Kye locked their lips with a hand gesture and stared straight ahead trying not to laugh. "How did I not know this?"

"It's not something I advertise." She pulled the truck back out and tried again.

And again.

And again.

Until Kye was full-on laughing and Florence was furious.

"We all have different skills, Kye!" Florence yelled when she finally got the truck to be relatively between the lines. "I want us to be able to make a quick getaway."

"Sure, I'm just guessing literally everyone on this property saw that and is definitely going to remember us and your truck." Kye had to wipe tears from their eyes as they climbed out of the cab.

"Get it together, Kye. We have to focus."

"Okay, okay," Kye said, still clutching their side and giggling. Florence kept glaring at them. "Okay, I'm done. I promise."

The two of them looked around the crowded parking lot and walked toward the combination art, history and gun museum.

"I spend all my time at the lake or in Guthrie. When do I ever need to back my truck in anywhere?" Florence added as they cut across the parking lot.

"Hey, I use a bicycle like ninety percent of the time. I'm impressed you got it as quick as you did." Kye grinned at her.

"Shush, you. We have some larceny to commit." She grinned back, and they stepped into the Lodge.

Chapter 16 Dani

After losing the cultist boat that was hunting her and swimming miles out of her way, Dani headed back to their family's lake house, hoping that Billy had followed the instructions she'd given him over the landline as soon as she'd returned to Kye's.

Much to her annoyance, and unsurprisingly, he had not.

"Dang it, Billy, I asked you to do one thing," Dani complained, hooking the bags she hadn't dropped onto the piers below the deck and sorting through them to see what she'd managed to salvage. Her self-confidence was at the bottom of the lake with the supplies she'd let go of. She wanted to let someone else be in charge, but Billy obviously wasn't that person.

"That's not true. You told me to do lots of things, and I am not even supposed to be in charge this week," he whined, crossing his arms and glaring at her in the water below the dock.

Behind him swam only a third of the kids. She was going to have to round up the rest, and none of them looked ready for a trek upriver.

"Things are more important than your video games, Billy." Dani was so annoyed. Of all the third-ish cousins in the world, he had to be the most obnoxious one in existence.

"Well, you never really tell me anything, so how am I even supposed to know that?" he argued back, readjusting his ball cap.

"Just get inside and grab the wet bags and make sure everyone is out here. We leave in five minutes. Dang it." She wanted to get them to safety before nightfall, and that was going to be difficult, knowing that the run-in she'd had with Muir wouldn't be the only threat to them as they traveled to the safety Grandmerm Sarnas could provide.

Dani scanned the lake for the hundredth time, looking for signs that the cultists were still following her. But, either the protection Sarnas put up was really good at hiding them, or Muir had never told the Church of the Flood the location of their land home because there were no cultists in sight. Nor had there ever been as far as she could tell.

"What's going on?" Gracie, one of the younger ones, swam up to Dani, scooping her into a hug.

"We just gotta go so you can meet the Grandmerm." Dani smoothed the girl's hair back out of her face and secured it with a band. "And we get to swim fast, so make sure you and your friends have your hair up and your vests cinched tight, okay?"

121

Gracie nodded and swam off to her pals. Dani watched as they took turns tying their hair back and making sure their laces were all snug. None of the kids were used to swimming in river depths, so the chances of snags on branches or rocks was high. They needed to get going as quickly as they could, but taking a few extra precautions was necessary.

Dani patted her own vest, double checking that everything she'd gathered was in place and hoping she wouldn't have to use the daggers Sarnas had gifted her. But feeling them secure in her vest comforted her.

Billy returned, and all the kids were accounted for. Dani did a second head count to double check, and all twelve of the little ones were there. It was strange to see so many of them in one place. Usually, they were much more spread throughout the lake, gathering occasionally to hang out or share a meal. But even then, it was just one or two families at a time, not every single kid.

"Okay everyone, we're going on a trip," Dani said, and the kids bubbled with anticipation. "It's really important that we stick close together like a proper school, and we're gonna swim fast, so get ready."

Again, there were murmurs of excitement. If there was one thing merfolk of all ages loved, it was swimming fast.

"When we get into the river network, I need you to pay extra close attention, okay? It's gonna take us most of the day to get to our destination. I don't want anyone to take a wrong turn or get lost."

Gracie raised her hand and asked what they were all wondering. "Where are we going?"

"To meet Grandmerm Sarnas."

This got even more of their attention, even Billy's.

"I don't think we're supposed to go that far without a grown-up." Gracie looked only slightly concerned, the excitement and curiosity overpowering her ingrained desire to not get in trouble.

"Well, I'm your grown-up now, and I'm taking you to a really rad even more grown up grown-up. So, you all need to remember how to be super respectful when we get to her, okay?"

The young ones nodded.

"Now pair up. I'm going to take the lead, and Billy is going to take up the back of the school."

Dani handed out a few small bags of supplies to some of the stronger swimmers and made sure they were secure enough to not snag easily but could be slipped out of if needed. They did final checks, and Dani swam up to Billy, putting her arms on his shoulders.

"I need you to take this seriously, Billy," she said.

And he nodded as she pressed one of the daggers Sarnas had given her into his hand.

"What's this for?" He examined the blade, turning it over in his palm.

"Just tuck it into your vest and try not to trip on it, okay?"

He did as she asked, his brow furrowed.

"Also, if anything happens to me, you have the map. Get the kids where they'll be safe."

He nodded again, his youthful face steely.

"And Billy? Don't trust Muir. No matter what he says."

The swim through the lake to the mouth where it branched into the river was uneventful and quick. They almost never swam in big pods because it was too risky and drew too much attention to them. Plus, it was easy to get caught up in the frenzy of swimming as a group.

If it hadn't been for the complete terror and dread in the pit of Dani's stomach, she might have even been having fun, but right now she was just focused on getting all the kids to Sarnas before Muir and the Church of the Flood could enact whatever deadly plans they had in mind. She kept glancing around, waiting for a boatload of redneck cultists to show up and try something.

The water was more churned up and murkier than normal in the lake, so the sudden change to the clearness of the riverbed was jarring.

What had been a relatively silent journey so far became a burst of loud chatter from the youngest, and Dani had to shush them. "I know it's exciting and most of us haven't spent much time upriver, but y'all have to try to keep quiet and stay focused. Let's go."

She could tell every single one of them would have rather spent the day in the sunny waters exploring and trying new plants and fish and looking for skipping stones, but they needed to make good time.

Every second they swam felt like she was racing fate.

So, when she saw him, it was like fate had caught up to her in a rush.

Muir's new tattoos were faintly glowing, though it was hard to tell for certain in the dappled water.

"Muir!" one of the younger ones shouted excitedly and made to swim toward him, but Dani took his arm gently but firmly and held him back.

The youngster gave her a confused look, and she shook her head. "That's not the Muir we know."

Billy swam up next to her.

"We don't wanna talk to you," he spat, and Dani was glad to see he'd at least paid enough attention to get the "Muir Bad" portion of her instructions.

125

"Let us pass, Muir." Dani held her arms out to show to the rest of the kids that they needed to stay put and wait for her to tell them what to do.

"Dani, Dani, Dani," Muir snarled. "All this tension between us. We're family."

"You haven't been family since you looped in with that cult. And besides, you're like my eighth cousin. That doesn't have to count for turds."

"I knew when I saw you here the other day that you weren't just here for fun. Where are you headed?"

So, he hadn't put it together that this was the way to the Grandmerm's. Hopefully, the kids—cough...Billy...cough cough—wouldn't give it away. She glanced at Billy sideways, and he didn't seem to be about to blow it.

"Just out on a swim, letting the kids do some exploring with us. To break up the monotony," Dani said, feeling the flimsiness of the lie as it came out of her mouth.

"Just out for a swim, huh?" Muir sneered. He swam a little closer. "Hey, Gracie, where are you headed?"

Dani swam forward to block him. "Stay the hell away from us, Muir. Don't even speak to her."

"Trying to keep me from my family? Dani, that is so unfair to everyone," he said loud enough for the whole group to hear. Then he whispered, so it only reached her ears, "I have lots of fun planned for all of them."

For a moment, Dani thought that maybe she and Billy could take him out together. Once upon a time when he was a scrawny teen, maybe. But whatever the cult was doing to him was like the instant potato type of steroids, and his tattooed chest bulged obscenely.

They probably started converting him by offering free protein powder, she thought, annoyed.

"What's going on?" One of the youngest swam up and reached his hand out to Dani. She took it and gave it a squeeze, not taking her eyes off Muir.

"Well, Dani here is trying to keep you from greatness." Muir bent down to make himself eye level with the child and offered a big, friendly smile.

But his sharkish eyes betrayed any semblance of goodwill.

"What's he talking about?" Gracie asked, and the murmurs around Dani rose as the young ones began whispering to each other.

"Muir is about to be in big, big trouble," Billy snarled, his neck fins flaring slightly.

"What did you do, Muir?" another kiddo asked.

"Only what I have been destined to do. We have power in us, children. Untapped and unparalleled power. It's up to us to use that power, or else what is the point?"

"You sound like such a smug dickhead, Muir." Billy rolled his eyes.

In a rush, Muir shot forward, his hand gripping Billy around the neck. "It would be best to watch your mouth around me, boy."

"Muir, stop!" Gracie yelled, and half of the littlest kids burst into tears.

Dani rushed up and knocked Muir's hand away. Billy swam a yard back, rubbing his throat. It wasn't actually possible to strangle a merfolk in the water, but it was still scary as heck, and the adrenaline coursed through Dani's scales.

"If you're done with your evil villain monologue, we're ready to go." She fingered the dagger tucked in the back of her vest and did not look away from him.

But she had no idea what to do next.

Chapter 17 Kye

"**W**ell, that's not subtle at all, is it?"

Kye and Florence were staring but trying not to stare at the giant harpoons hung above the massive stone fireplace, complete with a roaring fire even though it was warm enough outside that no one had any business lighting a fire indoors. But it added to the enormity and oppressive vibes the room was clearly going for.

Every spare inch of wall space was filled with the stuffed heads of animals from all over the world. Sometimes, it wasn't just the head either, but the whole animal.

"I don't even recognize all of these species." Kye's jaw dropped. "And I watch a lot of Animal Planet."

"I'm pretty sure that one is extinct." Florence pointed at an animal that was, in fact, extinct. Unironically due to over-hunting. Not surprisingly, the museum curators had left out that information on the little map handout.

Everything that wasn't an animal head was either made out of animal skin or covered with it. The rugs and the couches and the chairs all sported various hides.

It was unreal. If the wooden floors hadn't been visible, they'd have guessed they were walking on animal bones. Though it would not surprise either of them if the wood was from extinct tree species.

"One dude shot all of these little buddies?" Florence asked softly. They were almost alone in the space with the occasional small group milling about and also a docent who was doubling as a photographer where tourists could pay for a photo of their group with a twelve-foot-tall stuffed grizzly bear and its cubs.

The cubs part made them both very sad.

"Pretty sure it was in that, 'we have people go catch them ahead of time and chain them to a tree, then we hunt them' kinda way," Kye mused.

"This place is such a bummer."

"Agreed. Total bummer."

"Mr. Harold was definitely right about the location of the harpoons. Guess we don't need to wonder if we found the right ones."

Kye recognized the symbols etched into the weapons from the photographs Mr. Harold had shown them and the matching tattoos on Muir. As well as all the church signage. Because apparently, The Church of the Flood really liked a cohesive design aesthetic.

"Let's go get some food at the cafe and regroup," Kye suggested.

Florence gave an audible shudder when they got out the door.

"I'm not gonna feel guilty about this at all," Kye said as they made their way across the immaculate stone path lined with beautiful flower beds to the cafe which boasted overpriced box lunches and premade salads.

"My treat," Florence said. "You got the Sonic."

"Thanks." Kye ordered at the counter realizing they'd gotten off easy when the total came up.

Taking their lunches and drinks with them, they went outside and found a picnic table with some shade, far enough away from the other lunching groups that they weren't overly worried about being overheard while they made a plan.

The grounds were beautiful. Well-manicured but with lots of native plants and old-growth trees. Had they not just been inside the menagerie-turned-mausoleum, they might have enjoyed the views of the rolling hills and forests. Kye was willing to bet that the scenery in the fall when the leaves were changing would be spectacular, and it was unsurprising that the racist dude would take it for himself and his descendants.

"So, what do we think?" Kye asked, as they tore open the plastic cover on their salad and dumped the entire container of Ranch onto it.

"That all of this is bonkers and we should probably call our parents, but I can tell you're not gonna do that." Florence took a bite of her sandwich.

Kye shook their head. "At least we're on the right track and Mr. Harold and Sarnas are helping. It doesn't seem like a stretch that we might be able to use giant harpoons to stop a giant sea creature."

"Does it count as a sea creature if it's in freshwater?"

"Okay, giant lake creature, though I still hope we can find a way to avoid fighting this thing to begin with. It would be way better to just stop the cultists, right?"

Florence groaned. "True, but for now, I guess these harpoons are our best bet."

"I, for one, am not at all upset about taking something from this rich oil baron's estate." Kye said, and Florence agreed.

Four hours later, the museum was about to close, and Kye was hiding in a basement bathroom stall, middle school class ditching style—butt on the tank, feet on the seat, door cracked just enough to not look locked.

"Are you sure this is the best way?" Florence had asked.

Kye wasn't, but it made sense. They needed someone to take the harpoons, it needed to be when the grounds were closed, and they needed someone to get them back home eventually. Kye was by far the best at navigating nature in the dark. They were hoping to make it the two and a half miles or so to the main road before it was pitch black and were glad that the museum closed early enough to give them a chance at keeping the light.

Plus, one person disappearing in the crowd of everyone leaving and the other one who had been with them driving away was pretty easy to miss.

Throughout the few hours they'd been there, security didn't seem too tight. Mostly because the whole series of buildings was so far into the hills that it would be really hard to steal from. And as far as they could tell, there was only one road in and out.

So, thirty minutes before the museum closed, they'd split up.

"I'm glad I wore practical shoes for this," Kye said. "But I wish I'd brought a flashlight."

"Wouldn't that make you easier to spot?"

"Sure, but also, there are rattlesnakes out here."

"They mostly hunt during the day though, right?" Florence added unhelpfully.

"What? No, that is incorrect."

"Either way, be so careful," she said, giving Kye a hug. "I'll see you at the meeting place."

"If I'm not there by nine, you better not friggin' leave without me. I'm serious. You set up camp before you leave."

"I would never leave without you," she said, eyes wide as a cartoon character. She squeezed Kye in an even tighter hug.

"Yo, be cool," Kye said but gave Florence a tight squeeze back.

"See you soon. And make sure your phone is on do not disturb."

"Obviously." Kye rolled their eyes, but they double checked it anyway.

Kye kept busy on a crossword puzzle app on their phone, making sure the sound was completely off, until they heard the door swing open. Kye turned off the screen just in time as someone closing up for the night shut off the lights.

Florence sent a text saying she'd left the grounds.

The plan was for her to drive a few miles then turn around and drive back. She'd done this a few more times, trying not to look too terribly obvious, until she saw a museum worker come and lock the gate then take off in their car, leaving only the streetlamps and a small porch light on in the entrance kiosk.

It had been less than an hour of waiting on the toilet when Florence sent Kye a text saying things were as clear as they were probably gonna get.

"Here we go," they said in a whisper.

Kye pushed their way out of the bathroom as quietly as they could, listening for any sounds that might indicate a security guard was shuffling around out there.

They hadn't thought it possible, but the lodge was a thousand times creepier in the dusk. The only light streaming in was from yellow-tinted windows high up in the rafters, casting eerie shadows on all the animals, their glass eyes reflecting the setting sun.

"Please don't be bolted into the wall," Kye spoke softly to the harpoons as they quietly moved to a wooden ladder that held the skins of various breeds of cow.

They dragged the ladder, hides and all, across the room to the fireplace.

"Oof these are heavy," Kye muttered.

They'd decided to use the ladder because the hides were there specifically for people to touch, so if anyone dusted for prints, Kye's—along with like every single guest to come through—would be on it.

They leaned it up on the stones, slipped off their shoes, and were glad the rope and wood held as they climbed up to face the harpoons, certain that someone was going to burst in any second.

"Okay, dear stolen weapons, come to Kye." They reached for the first.

It came into their hands easily, having been laid on hooks and not bolted to the wall.

"That's right, danger stick, good girl," they said, resting it against the ladder.

It was taller than they were, and the jagged hook at the end gleamed in the little light that came through.

"You next, dear. Let's take you too." They gently lifted the matching set and rested them together.

Careful not to trip, Kye stepped down and pulled back on their sneakers, double knotting them, then replaced the ladder and made sure the hides were in place. They figured the longer it took anyone to figure out what the hell had happened, the better.

Walking as quietly as they could and carrying the harpoons, which were not extremely heavy but were awkwardly shaped, Kye went over to the side fire exit that was past the bathroom where they had been hiding. The door was the type that was always able to be opened from the inside for evacuation reasons.

It also happened to be facing away from the other buildings on the facility grounds and toward the woods where they were about to trudge two miles carrying these stolen weapons.

For a brief second, all they could think was, *Nope, forget it.*

Then they realized it was obviously already far too late to turn back.

Kye was going to kill Muir for dragging them all into this nonsense.

There was a good chance an alarm would sound no matter which door they opened, but if they wanted to get away with these harpoons, now was the time.

Pulling the over-sized hoodie they'd swiped from the gift shop up over their head as a makeshift disguise, Kye counted down from five and opened the door to the outside.

Chapter 18 Kye

Kye couldn't believe that no one was following them, but they'd been in the woods for a solid fifteen minutes, making what felt like good time, and even though they stopped to pause every ten seconds for the first few minutes, they didn't hear anyone. Ever since they'd closed the door behind them and made a beeline for the forest, they'd been waiting for an alarm to sound or to hear some night security guard yell at them. But it was just Kye, dragging their harpoon set behind them.

Well, not dragging, because they weren't a neanderthal.

But that might have been easier.

By Kye's estimation, they were about halfway to the meetup spot, and while they would be cutting it close to after sunset, they should make it to Florence before it was completely pitch black.

And it definitely would have gone that way.

Except they heard a loud sniff to their left.

They stilled for a moment, glancing through the brush and shadows. Nothing moved though, so they kept going. Until they heard it again.

Almost like a grunt. And then a splash.

"What the frack was that?" they muttered under their breath, pausing to listen.

Growing up in Oklahoma and spending so much time at the lake, Kye was used to certain types of wildlife, and they knew enough to stay relatively safe. But that would typically involve not walking alone in unfamiliar woods in the evening. The lake had its fair share of creatures roaming, such as foxes, wolves, and even the occasional mountain lion. Typically, the biggest threats were smaller more vicious and audacious animals like skunks and raccoons.

But there sure had been a lot of stuffed bears in that lodge.

Kye tried to shake the thought from their head and continued to walk as quickly and softly as they could, careful not to wake up any sleeping snakes and keeping the sun to their right.

If they didn't make good enough time, they'd have to use their phone flashlight and hope the GPS was working, even with such crummy reception. They were confident that they would be able to find the road but also needed to come out close enough to the meeting spot for Florence to pick them up.

They took a few more tentative steps and what was hopefully a shallow swamp came into view, sprawling out ahead of them.

"Cool, cool cool cool," Kye said. "This ought to be fun."

Hoping to spot someplace they could just hop over, they spent a few precious minutes walking up and down the edge of the marsh. Kye was solidly a lake person. Might not have been rational, but swamps and rivers kinda freaked them out.

"Not even a fallen log? Okay, just gonna cross it."

They hefted the harpoons and stepped into the algae-slick water, their tennis shoes making loud a squelching sound.

Then they heard the grunt again, this time much closer and from their other side.

In the setting sunlight, Kye could see eyes peering at them from the water. Much closer than they would have liked.

They got the distinct impression they were being hunted, or at least stalked, and it was not a feeling they enjoyed. Suddenly, it occurred to them that maybe that oil dude liked the opportunity to hunt on his own land and a few generations later, his prey might have made little predator babies of their own.

Trying their best not to think about leeches or water moccasins or other gross water creatures that lived in shallow and stagnant swamps, they took another tentative step into the mud and grimaced as it squished beneath their weight.

The sound of the stirring creatures following them was growing bolder.

There had also been a lot of alligator heads in that lodge.

"Nope," Kye muttered under their breath.

They wanted to walk the rest of the way across slowly, but like a ten-year-old taking the trash out at night, the impulse was to run, and when they did, they slipped on one of the slimy, algae-covered rocks and went down into the water on their knees with a grunt.

Scrambling to their feet, Kye used the harpoons to help them stand and swung around toward the approaching frigging water beasts that were looking more and more alligator shaped and ghostly white. Not looking away from the now way too many eyes, they reached down and felt a cut on their knee.

The alligators seemed to smell the blood in the water at the same time, and seconds later, the creatures, which had been keeping some distance, began a swimming race toward them.

Out of some instinct, Kye took a harpoon in each hand and pointed them toward the creatures.

If they were going to get eaten alive by alligators—or were they crocodiles? It really didn't matter at that point, even though they were sure that a quick Google search might have helped them figure out each different species' weakness, but there obviously wasn't time.

With a groan of frustration and annoyance that now their knees hurt, which would make it harder to run, Kye was certain they were about to be eaten in a swamp.

However, when they shifted the harpoon to their right hand, they felt a thrum and a vibration through it, and then it started glowing. For half a second, it felt like they were having a stress-induced hallucination and that the glow was just a reflection off the water.

But as the light got brighter, the animals stopped swimming. Almost as though they were frozen in place. Their eyes narrowed, and they simultaneously let out a ferocious and sustained hiss.

"What the heck." Kye looked from the harpoons to the creatures and back again.

The alligators stared unblinking at the glowing weapon, transfixed.

Kye slowly backed out of the swamp. "That's right, little lizards, watch the pretty light."

The animals' large bodies barely disturbed the water as they kept pace until Kye reached solid ground on the other side of the swampland. Then they all lined up right along the shore, eyes and long snouts peering at them.

"You stay, right there. Good Godzilla babies." Kye climbed out of the muck, doing their best to keep steady, not wanting to trip again.

The amount of teeth they could count now definitely shook their mind of the alligator vs. croc debate that had been silently going on in their head as they backed into the woods and away from the swampy area.

Once Kye had put some distance between themself and the army of reptiles, they turned around and started walking again as quick as they could, ignoring the sting in their knee, this time using the still-glowing harpoons to light their path.

Apparently, you don't really need many security guards if you have a platoon of hungry carnivores between any would-be robbers and freedom.

Kye's mantra for the next mile was "You can have a breakdown in a bit. You can have a breakdown in a bit."

When they finally reached the pavement, it was further west than they had planned, and they could see Florence's tail lights on in the distance, maybe a quarter mile down the road. They jogged despite their injuries because it felt like glowing eyes were still only one fallen tree log away. Kye felt like Ellie Sattler in Jurassic Park, limping away from the velociraptors.

"Let's get the heck outta here." Kye slammed the door shut as Florence cranked the engine.

"Are you okay?" she asked as Kye buckled themself up, and she pulled out onto the road.

Kye reached behind the seat and pulled out the first aid kit. They immediately grabbed some gauze and peroxide and had Florence pull over for a second while they tossed some medicine on their knees and bandaged them up.

"Are your hands cut too?" she asked as she drove exactly the speed limit back home.

"No, they're just messy." Kye wiped them on their jeans and realizing they were definitely shaking. "I may have a bit of a breakdown."

"Go for it." Florence took their hand in her own.

"There were, like, a lot of alligators just now."

"What?" Florence yelled, making herself jump.

"The good news is the harpoons we nabbed are definitely the right ones."

Chapter 19 Dani

Even though the water in the river flowed, Dani felt like her whole universe was at a standstill.

"Right, so you know I can't let you by." Muir floated in front of her, his bulky arms crossed.

"Fine." She crossed hers too, matching him posture for posture. "I'll stay, but let the young ones pass."

She gestured to usher them forward, but he held his hand up.

"Nah." His swollen, smug face was really ticking her off. More than it had in their youth. She thought for not the first time that he really was a total douche. "I'd rather we all stayed together. Family, friends, and all that."

"That doesn't really work for us." Billy swam up next to Dani and turned his baseball cap around so he could see properly. Dani was equal parts grateful and also annoyed that freaking Billy was her best ally at the moment.

"I was really hoping you'd say that." Muir snarled.

"What the heck?" Dani was beyond annoyed. "You were waiting for Billy to say something?"

"No, I mean both of you." Muir narrowed his eyes.

"Right so, what are you happy about?" Billy asked.

Dani was suddenly on alert. She sensed something unsettled in the water. Something shaking loose. Like the riverbed jostling and moving.

The rocks beneath them began to buckle, the silt bulging in parts.

As she looked into Muir's glazed over eyes, she realized he was ecstatic. And whatever was making him happy was waking up under the suddenly thin riverbed.

Muir grinned at them wickedly and took a deep breath. Then breathing out, he reached out his arms, and a swirl of river water spun around his outstretched limbs.

He had the audacity to wink at Dani.

And that was when the alligators shook the dirt and silt and stones from their heads and took notice of Dani and the rest of the merfolk school.

There wasn't time to make a plan.

But she had enough time to register that those alligators were foe, not friends. Any chance of a safe passage was most likely jeopardized because of the sudden appearance of an army of colossal reptiles with glowing eyes.

So yeah, not even the easy kind of alligator. Of course it was the glowy-eye type.

"What's your goal here Muir?" Dani snapped.

"To stop you," he said as though it was the simplest answer in the world.

"You mean to stop me from stopping you?" She decided now was the time to get clarification as she tilted her head toward Billy.

"Something like that." Muir snarled and lurched toward her just as Billy swept in and, tossing a clump of silt into his face, blocked Muir's vision temporarily.

"Swim!" Dani yelled, moving quickly toward the bank and gesturing toward the kids to follow suit.

The alligators that had emerged were on the edge of the river, and in the seconds they'd gained by Billy throwing the mud, Dani rolled herself to the south and used the sudden move and her body to block the three that had emerged nearest while the youngest merfolk sped past.

Thankfully, their school instincts had them pushing forward together almost as one. The two dozen young ones quickly swam out of Muir's reach, and Billy was close behind.

Dani didn't stop moving. She used her body and tail to both stir up the bed and push the alligators, which had not yet tried to attack her directly, back out of the way.

Her priority was getting the kids past Muir and upstream to where Sarnas was waiting.

And if that meant she had to take up the rear and apparently fight ten—no, twelve— demon alligators, so be it.

"Billy," Dani shouted after them, and he turned for a second, "swim friggin' fast."

He nodded briefly and sped away, the kids just ahead of him.

The alligators were swift. Oklahoma doesn't have many alligators, and the ones that are currently native to the state are super small. Like, could be considered cute or pet sized.

These were massive and pale white, their scales and eyes gleaming sinisterly in the shallow waters. Their powerful tails pushed them forward, and if it weren't for the fluid speed of the merfolk, the alligators could have easily caught them. Thankfully, the merfolk were faster and kept gaining distance between themselves and the alligators, Dani bringing up the rear.

Then, one of them got caught in the branches of a tree root system. It was Oli, one of the youngest, who missed the blockage and struggled to get loose.

"Help!" he cried, his eyes wide with fear and his neck fins flaring in his panic.

Billy spun around to tug at where he was wrapped in the current and branches.

"Go, Billy. Swim," Dani shouted, urging him on. If he could get the rest of them to safety, she'd have way less to worry about losing. She reached Oli. Part of his tail was wedged between two branches of a tree that was under the water.

Muir, seeing the struggle, slowed down and smirked at Dani, who spun around and, grabbing it from behind her vest, pulled the dagger out of its strap, pointing it at Muir.

"Back the hell off," Dani said.

She put herself between Muir and Oli, who was whimpering and tugging at his tail.

"You think you'll stop me with that little butter knife?" He was mocking her, and she was over it.

"No, but I know where the pointy part goes. I've seen *Game of Thrones*." Dani's brain was rapidly flipping between plans, and none of them ended easily. She didn't want to hurt anyone, but if Muir got any closer, she knew she was ready to protect Oli or any of the school.

So, when he did lunge, Dani's brain didn't really keep control, and some instinct kicked in. Relying on her gut, she swiped the dagger in a long arch, trying to cut him off. Instead of hitting flesh or scale, her arch cut through the water like she was pulling it through mud, and a hazy, green fog spread abruptly between her and Muir.

"What?" she wondered aloud.

But whatever the fog was, he wasn't coming through it, and she wasn't going to wait around. She spun and quickly used the dagger to free Oli's tailfin where it was caught.

Not letting go of Oli's hand, she sped upriver.

It felt like it took forever because he was so shaken up he could barely swim. After a minute, she wrapped him around her back and swam them both the last few miles to Sarnas, Oli clinging to her neck and whimpering.

"I want my parents," Oli cried into her hair.

She patted his hands. "Me too, kiddo."

The relief she felt when she crossed the protective barrier near Sarnas's home almost made her cry. It was even more distinct than the day before and Dani knew Sarnas had been busy reinforcing their protection in preparation for the arrival of the school. She gently passed Oli to Billy, who quickly distracted him with a joke.

Once the kids were settled, Dani and Billy met with Sarnas out of earshot of the kids.

"Now what?" Dani asked, trying to remain cool but internally freaking the heck out.

"Your land-walker friends met up with Mr. Harold to get instructions, right?" Sarnas asked, helping patch the part of Dani's tail where some of the stitches had opened up.

Everything was happening at such breakneck speed, Dani wasn't even sure when that had happened. Sarnas was using an algae poultice and what must have been some sort of binding magic because it stayed on Dani's scales like a bandage.

"Yes, they went to him." Dani tried not to hiss as the poultice heated up briefly.

"You're fine, child." Sarnas patted the spot, which, if anything, made it sting more. "The next step will be to retrieve the harpoon gun from Mr. Harold."

"Yeah, they are planning to meet him as soon as they get the harpoons," Dani said. "He gave them directions to his home where it's kept. I need to get back to them, but with Muir and the alligators blocking the way, I'm not sure I can."

Sarnas nodded. "How comfortable are you out of water?"

Dani thought about it. "I can manage a few hours." She'd been spending so much time on land lately, it was starting to wear on her.

"Good, and you, even younger one?" Sarnas looked at Billy. Dani noticed he didn't look quite as annoyed and bored as he usually did when keeping an eye on the school.

"Me?" he said. "Oh, I'm fine for a couple hours too."

"I think it's best if you both stay together. I will take care of the school. Mr. Harold will take you to wait for your friends." With little more explanation, Sarnas took off.

Billy looked at Dani, who shrugged.

"What happened back there?" He seemed more emo than usual, and Dani guessed he felt bad about leaving her and Oli.

"I'm not really sure," she admitted. "But I'm safe, and you did the right thing."

"I left you," he said glumly.

"No, you saved the rest of the school. I couldn't have gotten Oli out if you hadn't been protecting them while I did."

Billy thought about this for a few beats and then seemed to accept that he had made the right decision. The two of them returned to the children, who were playing a game of getting guppies to swim between designated stones and racing them.

Sarnas returned quickly and informed them that Mr. Harold would give them a ride to his home to wait for Florence and Kye.

"Are you sure I shouldn't stay here with the kids and you go with Mr. Harold?" Billy asked Sarnas. Dani felt a moment of sympathy and sort of wished she was only thirteen and could ask that question. But after the weird green fog, she knew it was her fight.

"I'm far too old for that, but stay if you want." Sarnas put her hand gently on his shoulder. "There is no shame in understanding one's own boundaries."

Dani squeezed his hand, knowing what he needed was a nudge. "I could use your company, Billy. It's gonna be wild out there, and your help getting the kids here safe was so important. But I understand if you can't."

He squeezed her hand then let it go, straightening his baseball cap, which Dani noticed he'd managed to hold onto during all the attacks and fleeing death and all that.

"Okay," he said. "I'll help."

"Keep the kids safe for us, okay?" Dani glanced over the riverbed at the group.

Sarnas nodded and held a hand to her chest. "With my life. Swim swiftly."

The two of them left but didn't go back the way they came. Rather, they traveled further upstream toward the USS Stonefish. Mr. Harold was waiting for them, his pickup truck backed up to the water down the slope where the submarine rested. It would have been much more unsettling to approach a human they'd never met before, but given the circumstances, Dani wasn't too pressed.

Sarnas could be trusted, and she clearly trusted Mr. Harold.

"You must be Dani." He tipped his hat and opened up the bed of the truck. He was on the shorter side, and his thick hair was gray. But his tanned arms looked strong, and he stood tall.

"Mr. Harold, pleased to meet you." She stretched her hand out of the water, and he bent down and shook it. "This is Billy."

He took Billy's hand as well.

"Pleasure to meet you, sir," Billy said.

"I'm sorry that the circumstances are what they are," Mr. Harold added.

"Us too," Dani said.

"Your friends should be at my home soon." Mr. Harold gave her a hand up into the bed of the truck, and she wondered for not the first time just how many rides she'd be taking on land this summer. Already she'd surpassed her record by taking more than one. He'd kindly laid out a rubber mat so they didn't have to lay on the bumpy truck bed, and there were several gallons of water secured behind a bungee cord near the cab.

Dani considered just how close Sarnas and he must be for him to have taken such thoughtful steps for their comfort. She was thinking that Sarnas and Mr. Harold probably hung out a lot more than she'd let on during their previous meetings.

"How far of a drive is it?" Billy asked, settling into the back, as Mr. Harold pulled a tarp over the bed.

"Not far, just down the road a bit. It won't get too bumpy though." As he closed the tarp, he added, "Hang in here. We'll be there soon, and I've got a swim tank at the house that's already filling up for y'all."

Yes, Dani thought, he and Sarnas were definitely closer than either of them let on. But given the importance of secrecy, that made sense.

They were not on the road for very long when he turned off into a small suburb. Dani was peeking out through a small slit in the tarp, and Billy had almost immediately fallen asleep. How that kid could nap through anything, Dani would never know.

Soon the truck slowed down to a crawl, and Dani could hear the crunch of gravel beneath the tires.

Then Mr. Harold whispered through the back cab window, "Y'all stay put and stay quiet."

Grateful that Billy remained asleep, Dani strained to hear what was happening and tried to keep completely still as Mr. Harold put the truck into park. Dani heard the brake being put on and the driver's door opening.

"Howdy, folks, how may I help you?"

Chapter 20 Dani

Dani strained to hear what was happening outside of the truck, but it was difficult, even with just the thin tarp over her and Billy.

"Mr. Harold," came a deep voice Dani didn't recognize, "we haven't had the chance to speak recently. Such a shame."

"Well, I'm gonna have to kindly ask you five folks to take your trucks and leave my property." Mr. Harold's voice was firm and steady.

Dani realized he was giving her information about what was happening outside of the truck with what he was saying.

Five folks seemed like a whole lot of strangers, and if they had more than one truck, that was extra scary. What did they want with him?

"We hear you asking that, but we have a feeling you might be trying to get in our way." This was a second voice, slightly higher pitched. Dani pictured a short, scowling woman, but she could have been completely off.

Either way, the sound was grating, and Dani felt chills as they spoke.

"I don't know about that and would just like to be left alone as much as anything, so move along. This is private property," Mr. Harold said more firmly.

"Based on what we found in your basement, you're not leaving well enough alone at all," said the original speaker in a tone that leaked venom behind its politeness.

Dani swore there was a crackle in the air at the mention of the basement. These cultists must have known way more than they had thought if they knew where the harpoon gun was kept. Hopefully, Florence and Kye wouldn't show up right in time to hand over the harpoons that made it work.

For the ten billionth time in her life, Dani wished that she had a cell phone and lived in a place with reception for it.

Billy began to stir, and she held her finger to her lips. Fortunately, he understood and stayed silent as the humans spoke. He mouthed, What's going on?

But Dani just shrugged and continued to listen.

"I didn't want to do this," Mr. Harold said, "but I'm gonna give you one more chance to get off of my property. There's nothing for you here."

"Well, see, we just don't quite believe you. Maybe you can let us have a look in your truck and you can let us into the basement vault, and we can all be happily on our way."

"That was your chance." Mr. Harold spoke in a firm and steady tone.

Dani felt the air change, and through the tarp, red light flashed. There was a popping sound but not a gunshot. It was more the sound of air going out of a hot-air balloon all at once. She couldn't help it and peeked through the gap in the tarp to see the cultists piling into their trucks, clearly yelling, though she couldn't hear it over the roar that followed the sound.

Both hands held open at his side, Mr. Harold was staring at them unblinkingly.

Red streaks of light and wind were corralling the cultists into their trucks like a dozen snakes. The glowing creatures were made of energy and lashed like whips, slamming doors closed on trucks and snapping at the backs of the fleeing cultists.

The cultists kicked up rocks and dirt as they tore down the gravel driveway in fear and haste.

When they were out of sight, Mr. Harold turned around, nodded at Dani, and then collapsed onto the ground in a heap.

"Oh silt." Dani ripped off the tarp and pushed herself to let the truck bed down so she could get out. "Billy, stay put."

She rushed over to Mr. Harold on the driveway, cringing a bit at the texture of the rocks across her wounded tail, but wasting no time.

"Mr. Harold." She got to him and felt for a pulse, which was thankfully there.

He was breathing, but it was shallow. As she felt around his head to make sure there were no major injuries she could find, a new presence rushed forward.

Dani stretched out her hand and yelled, "Stop right there."

But when she spun around and looked, the new person so closely resembled a young femme version of Mr. Harold that Dani immediately knew she must be his family. And she clearly had seen merfolk before because she didn't even blink as she rushed forward.

"I'm Sable. Richard is my uncle." The young woman knelt down and ran her arms across his forehead, similar to what Dani had just done. "What happened? I heard a noise."

"I'm Dani, and I'm not totally sure," she admitted. "He cast some sort of spell and got rid of those cultists though."

"Was it a big spell?" Sable narrowed her eyes, looking concerned.

"I don't really have a great frame of reference, but I'm gonna go out on a log and say, yes, it was a big spell."

Sable groaned. "I'm constantly telling him to take it easy. He's not cut out for this anymore."

159

"Cut out for what exactly?" Dani pressed.

But Sable was too focused on her unconscious uncle to answer, or else she was purposefully evading the question. "I'll be right back with the golf cart. He's probably not going to wake up for a few hours, and I need to get him inside."

Sable took off back around the house, and Billy popped his head up over the bed.

"Can I come out now?" He moved to the edge of the truck and hopped down.

Sable was back in a few moments, and with the somewhat awkward help of Dani and Billy, they got Mr. Harold into the back seat.

"We don't have to go far, but I'll take it from here. My partner doesn't exactly know about..." Sable gestured toward Dani and Billy.

Dani nodded.

"There's a swim tank around back, and most likely whatever Uncle did scared off whoever was here for quite a while. I assume it's that dang cult?" Sable wiped the dust off her hands and shook her head.

"Far as we know." Dani had about a trillion questions for Sable and a trillion and two for Mr. Harold, but the young woman seemed like such a no-nonsense being that Dani felt awkward about asking. Especially since her uncle was unconscious in the back of a golf cart.

"Well, I wish Uncle would let someone else handle it." Sable went to sit in the front seat. "I'll come back in a while and give y'all a ride back to the lake."

"We are actually meeting some friends here, hopefully soon, but thanks." Dani reached out and shook Sable's hand.

"I'll be back to check on you all anyway in a bit. Make yourself at home. But try your best to stay around back and outta sight." Sable gently put on the gas, and they watched her drive across the expansive lawn to the house next door.

Once she'd left, Dani turned to Billy. "Well, I guess we're going around back."

The two of them scooted around the side of the house, and sure enough, there was a big, metal trough almost full of water with a ramp leading up to it. There was plenty of room for them both, so they climbed up and slid in, sighing in relief at the cool water.

They'd only been there a few minutes when Bruno trotted out of the woods.

"What in the world, Bruno?" Dani scolded him. "You shouldn't be this far out."

He lumbered up onto the ramp and flopped himself down, his head resting within easy scratching reach of both Dani and Billy.

"How long do ya think it'll take for Kye and Florence to get here?" Billy had his head back and was floating in the tank like he'd been out of water for weeks.

"I have no idea, but I hope soon." She dunked her head under the water and took a deep breath.

It was not soon.

But Sable did show up with a stack of sandwiches and a couple of iced teas. Bruno barely opened an eye when she approached.

"Uncle is going to be fine," Sable said, "but he really shouldn't be pushing himself this way."

"What exactly happened?" Billy asked, finishing a sandwich in three bites and stuffing a huge handful of potato chips into his mouth.

"He cast a spell, and if he would just stay out of things and rest, this wouldn't happen and he wouldn't wear himself out." Sable took a bite of her sandwich.

"We needed his help," Dani said by way of apology. "We didn't know he would get hurt or, honestly, that he could even do what he did."

Sable nodded. "I'm just glad him and Sarnas aren't the only two working on whatever is happening right now. She shouldn't be pushing it either."

"Can you help us?" Billy asked, and Dani was grateful that she didn't have to swallow her pride to do the same.

"Not really. Not everyone is meant to be caught up in these things, and not everyone is equipped to actually make a difference."

"That seems rather fatalistic." Dani furrowed her brow.

But Sable just shrugged. "I'm going to go check on Uncle. You two are welcome to stay as long as you need. I'm guessing what he did will keep them away."

"It was nice to meet you." Billy tipped his baseball cap at her.

"You too. Stay safe." Sable gathered up the sandwich plates and made her way across the field.

"I should have asked for another sandwich," Billy said, and Dani laughed, dunking his head underwater. She was really glad he was with her. But she also really hoped that Kye and Florence would get there soon.

Chapter 21 Kye

The sky was fully dark by the time Florence turned onto the road leading to Mr. Harold's house. There was an eerie, green glow across the horizon toward the direction of the lake that neither of them had seen before. It looked a lot like the sky before a tornado, but the color was the wrong shade of green and the sun had fully set.

Kye and Florence rode with the windows down, even though it was a bit chilly with the breeze. It felt good on Kye's skin and was helping to calm them down after their alligator heavy trek through the woods.

"Take the next left," Kye instructed, using their phone to light up the map that Mr. Harold had drawn for them. They turned onto a smaller driveway and could see a few other homes across well-kept lawns as the headlights turned toward his house.

When they drove up, however, they noticed immediately that his truck was parked at an odd angle and there was a tarp laying in the driveway. Based on the immaculately landscaped walkways and gardens and flowerpots across the porch, random tarps strewn about did not seem typical for Mr. Harold.

"We're sure this is the right house?" Florence asked, putting the truck into park.

"Yep, definitely the right house." Kye opened up the truck door and stepped out.

"Mr. Harold?" Florence called, stepping out of the truck as well but leaving the headlights on to give them a better view of the house.

"Mr. Harold?" Kye repeated, walking up and knocking on the door but to no reply. "The lights are off inside."

Then, Kye held up their hand at the sound of a splash from around the back of the house.

"Ugh, Bruno, get out of here," came a voice.

"Dani?" Kye hurried around the back and came upon Dani, Billy, and a very soggy Bruno all crammed in a metal swim tank.

"Kye, thank goodness. Call off your beast." Dani laughed.

"Bruno, what on earth are you doing? Get out of there," Kye scolded, gesturing for Bruno to get out at the ramp.

He took his sweet time but eventually climbed out, shaking and spraying all of them with soaked dog water.

"Eww. Bruno, why?" Kye wiped at their face.

Bruno, clearly unfazed, trotted off back around to the front of the house.

"Don't go far," Kye called.

He turned and glanced back at them then continued on with a slight wag of his tail.

Kye turned back to Dani and Billy. "What are y'all doing here? Where's Mr. Harold?"

Dani and Billy briefly described what had happened with Muir blocking their way back to the lake and then told them about when Mr. Harold cast the spell, and Kye and Florence listened, eyes wide.

"Holy smokes." Kye was actually pretty jealous that they'd missed seeing it. Though it sounded really scary, it also sounded really badass.

"So now we're waiting for you so we can hopefully figure out the harpoon gun situation. We didn't want to risk going in on our own since we'll probably need legs to get into the basement." Dani gestured to Kye's and noticed the scrapes and bandages. "Wait, what happened to you?"

"I'll fill you in later, but we should probably get going," Kye said then stopped. "Wait, what happened to you? Why is your tail covered in grass?"

"You're not gonna believe it," Billy chimed in and took a breath like he was about to launch into an epic tale.

Dani held up a hand. "We'll fill you in later too, but Kye is right—we need to get moving."

"So, we're just gonna go ahead and assume there's no alligators in the basement?" Florence put her hand on her hips. "I am not a fan of the miscommunication trope, and not telling each other about friggin' alligators seems like an oversight."

"Wait, your story has alligators too?" Billy was far too cheerful about that fact.

"Okay, so we all know there might be more alligators. Let's get into this basement because I'm so tired I might fall asleep right here and let y'all handle the apocalypse." Dani handed Kye a key she'd gotten from Sable. "This opens up the basement. The door is back here."

Near the tank, there was a thick, wooden door without windows that opened right away when Kye slid the key into the lock and turned it with a satisfying click.

"Be careful." Dani leaned forward from the tank and placed a hand on Kye's arm.

At the touch, the cool night air seemed to warm around Kye. "We will."

Kye and Florence walked down the wooden stairs slowly, using the flashlight from Kye's cell phone, though it was about to die so the plan was to find the light switch soon. An eerie glow was coming through the ceiling, casting dim shadows all across the space.

"This is my worst nightmare," Florence whispered.

They shushed her. Right as *their* worst nightmare happened and something grabbed their ankle from between the stairs.

Kye screamed and yanked their foot away, stumbling down the last four steps, their flashlight clattering to the ground. Florence screeched as the figure continued to reach through the gap in the stairs, trying to trip her. She stomped on its hand as hard as she could, and Kye heard what sounded like bones crunching under her boots.

The person howled in pain and anger and scrambled to get out from where they had been hiding behind the stairs.

In the dim light, Kye could see the flash of a knife in the hand of the cloaked person.

"Watch out!" Florence took the last few steps down into the basement, knocking into the figure.

Kye lunged from where they had stumbled and tripped the attacker as they tried pushing past them to reach the stairs, unbalanced by Florence's shove. Kye wasn't going to let a knife-wielding baddie get past them to where Dani and Billy were waiting upstairs and, in an adrenaline-fueled moment, knocked the knife out of the figure's hand and pushed them with more strength than they knew they had.

A pulse of green flashed, and the person went flying a few yards into the opposite wall, landing on the ground with a thud.

Just then, the lights in the basement clicked on.

"Whoa," Florence said. She had found a dangling light switch.

Kye thought she was commenting on the still faint green of their hands, but a quick glance told them, that no, she was actually commenting on the state of the basement. Kye scanned the space quickly and saw a mess that looked like someone had dumped out all the shelves in a Home Depot, but then returned their focus to the person at their feet, who was apparently trying to scootch away and was getting tripped up by the tangle of robes around them.

"I'm gonna need you to not wiggle." Kye stepped on their cloak so they couldn't move further and knelt down.

"You'll never break me." The person spat. Kye realize"How about you?" looked really familiar.

They were about the same age as Kye and had long, brown hair tied in messy braids that hung down their chest. Under the cloak, they were wearing grubby overalls and what looked like a Vacation Bible School T-shirt with the Church of the Flood logo on it.

That was dark, Kye thought.

"What? I'm not going to try to break you," Kye finally registered what they'd said. "What's your name?"

"Tara," they answered in a huff as though Kye was the one greatly inconveniencing them.

"Well, I'm Kye. My pronouns are they/them. Would you like to share yours?"

Tara looked at them with narrowed eyes then shrugged. "She/her."

"Okay. Now that introductions are out of the way, want to tell us what you're doing here and why you're all alone?"

She let out another huff. Apparently, that was how she talked. Kye was already annoyed with her, knife wielding aside. Without meaning to, Tara's gaze flicked over to a spot above where Florence was standing.

"They cut a hole in the ceiling." Florence pointed to a large opening where Kye could see parts of what they both guessed was Mr. Harold's living room. Chunks of hardwood floor looked like they had been pried up with a crowbar, and directly under the hole was a crumpled-up rope ladder.

"Are you just stuck down here?" Kye said. "You know there's a door, right?"

Tara huffed, yet again. "Yes, I know there's a door. I just couldn't open it."

170

From the top of the stairs, Dani called down, "Y'all okay down there? What happened?"

"We have company," Florence hollered back up at her.

"What do you mean you can't open it? Looks like y'all made quick work of going through the floor." Kye pointed out.

"Door's different" was all Tara cared to elaborate.

That was when Kye noticed Tara's hand. Where Florence had stomped it, there was swelling, and a few of her fingers seemed bent at incredibly wrong angles.

"I think you need to get to a doctor, right away." Kye gestured to the hand that Tara hadn't seemed to notice. She looked down and scowled.

"I'm not going to a doctor. We don't believe in that." She spat and shoved her hand into her cloak pocket in such a rough way that both Kye and Florence flinched. Tara didn't so much as make a face, like the hand wasn't hurting her at all.

"Oh-kay." Kye stood, not really knowing what to do. Most of the adrenaline had worn off, and they were frankly extremely tired. "Florence, grab those ratchet straps."

She looked at them questioningly.

"I'm just gonna tie her up long enough for us to handle the you-know-what." Kye figured Tara knew exactly what they were in the basement for but no need to advertise it. "We'll let her go when we're done."

"Who is it?" Billy called down from the top of the stairs.

"She says her name is Tara," Florence answered, getting the straps and handing them to Kye. "You just gonna let her watch us do stuff?"

"Good point." So, they put Tara in a lawn chair facing the wall. The straps were loose enough that they wouldn't hurt her but tight enough that she shouldn't be able to just hop out and run.

Only then did Kye shift focus enough to take in what was before them.

A floor-to-ceiling vault stretched across a whole wall.

"This may take a while, y'all." Florence started up the stairs. "But there's a giant hole if you wanna hang out and watch while we figure it out."

"Sounds good," Dani said, and she and Billy got out of the tank.

"I'm gonna go make a pot of coffee," Florence called down the stairs while Kye stood, arms crossed, staring at the barrier.

Chapter 22 Kye

"It's like they robbed a pawnshop dumpster." Florence nudged the chainsaw with her shoe and took a sip of coffee. The chain had fallen off, and the blade was bent at an odd angle, burn marks charred the broken teeth.

She had filled Dani and Billy in on what had happened, and they made their way through the house so they could watch on their bellies from the hole in the ceiling. The basement stairs were too old to risk going down, but they wanted to see what was happening. From what they'd gathered, the cultists had spent quite a few hours throwing the kitchen sink of tools at the wall to no avail. There were barely any scratches in the steel-blue paint.

"I'm surprised they didn't blow all the fuses in the house." Kye moved a broken jackhammer out of the way of the door.

"We use battery powered tools, duh." Tara rolled her eyes. None of them could actually see her eyes since she still face the corner, but it was obvious.

"Wait, Tara?" Dani called down from the hole in the ceiling.

"Dani?" Tara answered, twisting to turn around to see Dani peeking through the hole.

"Y'all know each other?" Kye was taken aback. And confused.

"Well, yeah, kinda." Dani grimaced.

"How?" Billy and Florence asked at the same time.

"Tara?" Dani asked in a way that seemed to Kye like she was asking for permission.

"Fine, go ahead and tell them. It's not like any of y'all are gonna live past the next couple days anyway."

"Firstly, rude." Kye held a finger up at Tara. "Secondly, what's going on?"

Dani shrugged. "Tara and I were in a lot of the same classes for our GEDs. We had a group project we worked on together last semester."

"Wait, what?" Billy turned to Dani, shocked. "How'd you manage that? Why don't I get to go to school?"

"Yes, please answer him." Tara gave up on trying to turn and just spoke toward the corner. "Because I definitely didn't get merfolk vibes from you, and we spent a lot of time on video calls."

"Filters." Dani shrugged, and Kye looked up at her with amazement. "Okay, but what does a cultist who's about to bring the end of the world need with a GED?"

Tara stiffened and hesitated. "It gets pretty boring out here in the country. I just wanted something to pass the time."

That answer actually made a lot of sense to the group, so they didn't press her further.

"Well, anyway. Now that this really strange overlapping of worlds is over, we should probably try and open up this thing." Kye left from where they had been standing near Tara and went to examine the vault.

The door resembled the passageway between two sections of a submarine. There was a large, circular handle that presumably opened up the hatch into the next section where the harpoon gun was stored according to Mr. Harold's niece. She had no idea how to open it, but had seen the inside a couple of times. Unfortunately, that was all the help she could give and had left to go watch over her uncle again.

Various runes and symbols were stamped into the metal.

"Those look kinda like the daggers Sarnas gave me," Dani pointed out.

"I was thinking the same thing," Kye agreed.

"Here, catch." Dani gently dropped one of the daggers hilt first, and Kye caught it with ease in the hand that wasn't holding a mug of coffee. Kye hadn't taken the time to study it as closely as Dani had, but the hilt had similar symbols and runes worked into the handle. Giving Florence a shrug, Kye stepped closer to the wall and sort of poked at the vault with the dagger.

They felt ridiculous, and nothing happened.

"You don't think you need to like, cut yourself, do you?" Florence grimaced and said it in a whisper.

"I mean, the harpoons did do that thing when I cut my knees?" Kye really didn't want to cut anything though, so they kept poking at the wall in various places.

Tara let out a condescending laugh. "Not so easy, is it?"

"Don't be smug, Tara." Kye scowled. "You're the one whose pals left her stuck in a basement like bait."

"Oh silt." Dani must have had the same thought as Kye. They were definitely on the same page thinking that Tara might be actual bait. There was a good chance the whole broken ladder thing was a ploy and truckloads of cultists would be back any minute.

Tara laughed again. "Running out of time to save the world?"

Kye was getting really fed up with Tara's attitude and, for a moment, wished they had it in them to render someone unconscious. It also bothered them a little more than it should have that Tara knew all about Dani's schooling before Kye did.

They took a step forward and tried in vain to turn the wheel for about the hundredth time.

"You're never gonna get it in time. You might as well give up," Tara taunted. "Except for you two up there. We could use you."

Now Kye was feeling well past annoyed and bordering on angry.

"What was that?" they asked, stepping around Tara so they could look her in the eye and point the dagger at her in a way that felt menacing and natural.

"Just saying, your merfolk companions are useful. We like using them." The way she said it was really pissing off Kye.

"Stop talking," they said and moved to walk away.

"Even if I stop talking, you know it's true. They're much more useful than you could ever be. And we'll get them to help us one way or another. Everyone comes to the Flood eventually."

Kye knew in their bones that they wouldn't let that happen. That Dani and her family and people would be safe. That the towns below the dam and the homes above the dam would be safe from the Flood and anything else that threatened them.

Heat grew in their gut.

When they looked down, their hands were doing that glowing thing, and it definitely wasn't in their head, based on the look Florence was giving them.

Any bit of doubt was gone, and Kye walked back to the vault one more time, gripping the wheel with both hands.

It rotated and then swung open with a clang as smoothly as any refrigerator door.

"Holy mackerel." Florence watched the glow fade from Kye's palms as quickly as it had started.

Billy let out a whoop. "Rad, Kye!"

"Wait, what happened?" Tara strained against the ratchet straps, trying to turn around. "What happened?"

"We got into the vault. Now shush, you naysayer." Florence stepped through the large opening first.

"Keep an eye on Tara," Kye called up to Dani, who was watching them with a steady look on her face.

The inside of the vault was a sight to behold, and Kye snapped a few photos with their phone to show to Dani and Billy later.

The back wall was straight out of the "super hero who has a fancy day job and needs to store all their weapons in a hidden compartment that's all organized and shiny" handbook. Total Bruce Wayne money for the set up too. Not someone broke like Jessica Jones.

The harpoon gun was mounted in the middle of the room, but Kye swerved around it and went directly to the back wall. There were dozens of different types of weapons. Some looked ancient, like a bow and quiver set. Others looked brand new, like a row of tiny knives and a crossbow.

"For someone who seems so chill, Mr. Harold sure does have quite the armory," Kye pointed out. They were tempted to pick up and hold all the weapons, but there wasn't time to examine them all.

The other two walls were not as impressive, but were stacked with boxes similar to the ones in Mr. Harold's conference room at the USS Stonefish. The harpoon gun was partly disassembled, the mount and the firing portion on a table off to the side. Without the base, it looked a lot like a rocket launcher.

"Think we can figure out how to put it together?" Florence wondered aloud.

But Kye wasn't worried. They could practically see LEGO-quality instructions on how to assemble it in their head. "Shouldn't be a problem." They picked up one of the parts, surprised at how lightweight it felt in their hands. "I'm gonna take this part to the truck."

Dani met them around the front when they got up the stairs and around the house.

Jes McCutchen

"I think we should hurry." She nodded toward the road. "They could be back any minute."

Kye noticed that the fog Mr. Harold left had faded to almost nothing and agreed. "I'll go get Florence and the rest of the pieces."

"What are you gonna do with Tara?" Dani had a concerned look on her face.

Kye's brow furrowed. They definitely didn't want to deal with a captive. "I hadn't really thought about it. Probably just let her go."

"Her people might get her killed," Dani pointed out.

"She also did just mention that she was totally fine with their plan to get all of us un-alived, so I'm not too worried about her." Kye was itching to get back and assemble the harpoon gun, and this Tara character was adding one more roadblock.

"Well, we can't exactly leave her tied up until this ends. She may never get out of that basement." Dani crossed her arms and gave Kye a look that said, *You better come up with something else.*

"She has her people. They'll get her out. She's choosing to do what they ask."

"You saw her shirt. She probably hasn't ever had a choice in being part of this. And I don't think they knew she was even taking classes. She was probably having to sneak around." Dani was always more empathetic than Kye, but it seemed like this was

Kye's responsibility to sort, even though Dani and Tara apparently went way back.

Kye wasn't sure what response Dani was looking for. And they were weary with the non-stop decision making. "Well, I guess I'll give her a choice now?"

Dani nodded and got into the bed of the truck.

"I'll send Billy out too." Kye made their way back around the house and into the basement, where Florence was still looking through the vault.

"Check these out." She pointed.

One of the walls held a bulletin board which was lined with images. Blurry and obviously taken with real film cameras ages ago. But the general vibe was this demon cephalopod was going to really mess some stuff up.

"We gotta go." Kye grabbed the other two parts of the harpoon gun and tipped their head to the door. Florence snapped a couple more photos on her phone and followed. She tried to close the door, but it wouldn't budge.

However, Kye, arms full, used their hip, and it swung shut with ease, the handle spinning itself locked.

"Do you have super strength now?" Florence put her hands on her hips.

"I have no freaking clue." Kye walked over to Tara. "You have a choice. You can come with us, and we can try and rehabilitate you out of this cult situation. Or we can leave you down here, and you can climb out or wait for your pals."

"I'm obviously not going with you." Tara huffed, blowing her bangs out of her eyes.

"Should we try to be a little more convincing than that?" Florence looked at Tara with pity.

"We don't have time for this. Let's just untie her and bail." Kye shifted the weapon and loosened the ratchet straps enough that she would be able to get out soon.

Kye and Florence were at the top of the stairs when they heard Tara.

"Wait," she said.

They both turned, wondering if she'd changed her mind, Kye halfway hoping she hadn't.

"Can y'all please leave the light on?"

Chapter 23 Dani

Dani and Billy loaded into the bed of Florence's truck, which, Dani noticed, was not nearly as comfortable as Mr. Harold's had been. The two of them sat between the pieces of the harpoon gun and the harpoons themselves, low against the cab. But they didn't bother with the tarp. It was late enough out that no one would be able to see them with any clarity.

The foggy mist that had covered the edges of the property was almost completely faded now, and the streetlights at the end of the driveway were fully visible.

"Hurry up, you two," Billy called to the others as he settled in, getting as comfortable as he could with the nearly full truck bed. He'd probably be asleep before they left the driveway.

Florence and Kye were wrapping up inside and had just closed the front door of Mr. Harold's house when the lights from several vehicles appeared at the end of his driveway.

"Folks, we may have a problem." Dani peered down the road.

Rather than large trucks, this time the visitors were on four-wheelers flashing their lights threateningly. Which meant that they might not be as powerful but they could drive just about anywhere so long as they knew the way.

It wasn't going to help that Florence's truck was so weighed down between the two merfolk and the entire harpoon rig.

Kye and Florence rushed down the last of the steps and into the cab.

"What are they waiting for?" Florence started the truck and put on the headlights, which didn't reach quite as far as where the cultists waited on their vehicles.

"I bet the spell Mr. H. cast is going to wear off, if it hasn't already." Kye buckled up. "Worst case scenario, they're here for us. Best case, to get Tara out of the basement."

"What should we do?" Florence let off the emergency brake, but still had the truck in park.

"I think we have to go through them." Dani grimaced.

"But they're packed so close together," Florence pointed out with a whine.

"It's gonna be a game of chicken then." Kye grabbed the dashboard.

"I'm not playing chicken with my baby." Florence gave her truck a pat.

"We don't have much choice. They can't get the harpoon and harpoon gun. And we can't let them get to Mr. H. If they do, we're in big trouble." They gave Florence an apologetic smile.

"Also, we noticed it was your truck and not us that you were worried about. Kye was just too nice to point it out," Dani said through the window in the cab.

"It's not my truck's fault she's caught up in all this." Florence put it into drive. "You two hold on tight back there."

They didn't have enough bungee cords to strap both the harpoon rig and the merfolk down, so it was going to get hairy.

Dani looked over at Billy. "You ready?"

He nodded. "Yep. Florence has got this."

Dani was becoming more and more grateful that Sarnas had encouraged him to go with her.

"Here we go." Florence revved the engine and took off straight toward the line of menacing-looking four-wheelers.

Dani almost laughed at the situation. If someone had told her the day Florence got the truck that she'd someday be driving it full speed at a bunch of cultists, she never would have believed it.

The dust kicked up immediately, and Dani wished she'd brought more water. Being out of the lake was one thing, but being caught in dusty gravel air that was stagnant and humid was something else. She closed her eyes and reached a hand to hold onto the side of the truck as Florence laid on the horn.

The cultists had obviously moved because, after counting to ten in her head, Dani still hadn't felt the truck hit anything massive or metal or fleshy, and angry yells echoed down the road at them as the cultists turned their vehicles around and gave chase.

Seconds later, the truck was on smooth pavement, and Florence was flooring it down the road. The dust from the drive cleared, and Dani could see the half dozen cultists going full speed on their tails. They'd apparently not taken the time to go free Tara, and Dani was grateful that her friends were so much better than this pile of farts.

But the cultists were gaining on them.

"How are they catching up so fast?" Dani called through the cab window.

"Magic powers? I don't know." Kye had turned around and was watching them out the back.

"Well, we need to lose them somehow," Florence shouted. The road was winding, but there were not any random turn-offs they could take since they were so far out into the country. If they turned down the wrong way, they were more likely than not to hit a dead end or a farm or a lake.

If they'd been closer to home, Kye probably could have told Florence where to drive, but they were far from areas they were familiar with.

At this rate, the cultists would catch up well before they made it to Kye's property and behind the protective wards.

"We don't have to lose them," Dani said. "We just have to slow them down."

She wondered briefly why there hadn't been similar wards on Mr. Harold's property, and she felt a pang of guilt at the thought that maybe he hadn't needed the until she and her friends had led the cultists there.

"Hold these for me." Kye reached through the window and handed Dani a small rolled up canvas pouch. "Be careful you don't cut yourself."

"Knives? Are these throwing knives? Why do you have these?" she shouted over the wind and engine sounds as she opened up the bundle and looked inside.

"I kinda borrowed them from Mr. H.?" Kye had rolled down their window and, to Dani's horror, was now climbing out of it.

"What the blazes are you doing?" Florence swerved and then jerked the truck back onto the road when Kye screeched and clutched the side mirror to stay on.

187

"Stop driving so wiggly," Kye said. "I've gotta get in the back."

"Hold these." Dani handed the pile of knives to Billy, who looked frankly impressed by Kye. She took Kye's hands, pulling them into the back of the truck with an undignified plop as Florence took a sharp corner, thankfully throwing Kye the correct direction into, not out of, the truck bed.

"Thanks." Kye grinned at Dani from on top of her, where they'd landed. Kye's face was roguish, and their eyes gleamed with excitement. They were enjoying this, Dani realized with a flush.

Taking the knives from Billy, Kye stood up in the back of the truck and aimed.

Dani grabbed Kye's ankle. "Wait. Don't hurt them."

"Just gonna pop their tires."

Kye's hand glowed as it had in the basement, and they threw one of the knives at the closest cultist. It missed, but their rear tire kicked it up and the knife spun into one of the ones behind it. With a loud pop and a skid, there was suddenly one less cultist to fuss with at the moment.

Billy let out a whoop, and Dani had to admit she was also impressed.

The next two knives hit their marks, and the two front riders were left behind. One was thrown from their vehicle into the side of the road, but if they were injured, it wasn't grave enough to keep them off their feet or from shaking their fists in the light of their still-running four-wheelers. Dani heard them yelling at the others to keep going and catch up with the escaping truck.

They were almost home, and Kye still had two throwing knives. But some of the adrenaline seemed to have left them, and the last two throws went wide.

It didn't matter though because as soon as they crossed the barrier onto Kye's land, the protection kicked in and the three remaining four-wheelers skidded to a stop before they crashed into it.

"That thing sure is handy." Dani reached out her hand and helped Kye find a seat among the weaponry.

"Wish I hadn't wasted my knives." Kye looked forlorn.

"We made it, didn't we?" Dani gave their hand a squeeze and nodded toward the lake house as Florence pulled the truck in.

"True. But they were really cool and I only got to have them for like twenty minutes."

Florence parked, and they all got out of the truck and headed to the dock, where Dani and Billy were relieved to dive into the cool depths. They were all very hungry so after she and Billy had been in the water a few minutes, Florence and Kye met them with piles of random snacks.

"I'm sorry. I don't even have the energy to make a sandwich right now." Florence sat down heavily and took a giant scoop of peanut butter out of the jar with a spoon.

"No apologies necessary." Dani dug directly into the Tupperware of leftover potato salad with the fork Kye handed her.

They all shoveled food for a few minutes in relative silence. Everyone on the brink of total exhaustion but buzzing with left over adrenaline. The meal seemed to mellow everyone but Kye, who kept bouncing on the balls of their feet and crunching on whatever bites Florence handed them.

Bruno trotted up soon after the first bag of chips was opened and was given his fair share of nibbles.

"I'll feed you properly in a minute." Kye paused their pacing to scratch behind his ears.

"So, I think we need to all try and get some sleep." Dani did a stretch and back flip in the water, shaking her jumpy muscles loose.

"That's a good idea." Kye was pacing on the narrow planks. If they were able to fall asleep, it would be a small miracle. "Tomorrow morning, I'm going to the sunrise service with the Flood."

"What?" Dani and Florence asked at once.

"We have to at least give it a shot." Their nervous energy was distracting everyone. "They have it every Wednesday. I should go."

"Right, so we're gonna put a pin in that discussion until tomorrow morning." Florence crossed her arms and gave them all a look that was no-nonsense. "Come on. We need showers and sleep."

She put her arm on Kye's elbow.

"You two gonna be safe down here?" Kye asked as they let Florence lead them up the dock.

"Safe as any of us can be." Dani gave what she hoped was a reassuring smile. "I'm just glad we don't have to worry about the school tonight."

"Same, though I kind of already miss them," Billy admitted, pulling his baseball cap slightly over his eyes as if to remind them he was cool.

"We'll see you in the morning." Florence steered herself and Kye up to the house.

Billy turned to Dani. "Think you'll be able to sleep?"

"No. But you go on ahead. I'll keep watch."

He slipped under the dock, and she floated on her back, staring at the sky.

Chapter 24 Dani

"What are you doing?" Dani asked as Kye made their way back down to the small dock less than an hour later.

"I figured I may as well sleep out here and keep you company," Kye said, setting the lantern they'd brought down and unrolling the sleeping bag and bedroll they'd pulled from the garage.

"Why?" Dani asked, moving toward the side of the dock where Kye was setting up and resting her elbows on the wood. She could tell Kye had showered, the smell of clean soap still lingering on their skin.

"Just usual near-death things, you know."

"Oh, right, sure," Dani said, ducking her head under the water and coming back up with six perfect skipping stones. She laid them next to the lantern.

"It always amazes me that you can find those in the dark," Kye said, picking up one of the stones and hefting it from one hand to the other.

"For all you know, I have piles stashed around here for just this type of moment and you just think I see in the dark."

Kye rolled their eyes. While the merfolk had super sensitive nerve endings that could feel the pressure changes caused by things moving in the water like boats or fish, Dani was just really good at feeling around the edge of the lake for the smooth stones that could go the furthest when thrown correctly.

"Where's Billy?" Kye asked. They couldn't see him in the dim light.

"He's tucked in under that side of the dock," Dani said, nodding to the opposite end.

When they were at home, they slept in underwater hammocks to keep from floating around and bumping into stuff. Sort of like how astronauts sleep. So, it made sense that they would choose to sleep under the dock, where there was wood and bars to help keep them in place for the night.

Dani had told Kye horror stories about what equated to sleepwalking by merfolk. It was the main reason there are even rumors about their presence. Thankfully, most people out on the lake at night were inebriated to some extent, so most folks just chalked it up to seeing things.

"Well, best two out of three gets the first drink," Kye said, bringing out a bottle of whiskey they'd nicked from the pantry on their way back.

"Just grab a stone." Dani laughed.

Kye stood at the edge of the dock. They hefted the stone in their right hand, feeling the smooth, round edges.

"Okay, shush," they hushed Dani who had moved to tread water parallel to them.

"You know I don't need to hear it," Dani said.

"Yeah, but I don't trust you not to cheat, so I have to count myself," Kye huffed.

It was like they were twelve again. Ignoring the others who had long since given up on skipping stones. But match after match, Kye and Dani would tie, or one would win and the other demand a rematch until the rest of them shouted it was time to eat lunch and to cut it out. Dani rolled her eyes, knowing full well that Kye didn't actually think she'd cheat, but also that they were going to count anyway.

Their part of the lake was usually great for skipping stones, but behind the protective barrier it was almost too calm.

"Wait." Dani held up her hand and put her head under the water. When she came back up, Kye was watching her intently. "The water is much calmer than it has been. Even on this side of the barrier."

"I'm kinda getting very 'don't disturb the water vibes tonight' too." Kye hesitated with their next throw.

Dani paused for a second. "There's nothing abnormal that I can tell. But it's like the wards are bracing for what is coming."

"Call it a draw?" Kye handed Dani the bottle.

"You first." Dani waved it off.

"You earned it." Kye took a seat cross-legged on the sleeping bag, the light from the lantern casting a small ring that reached half in the water, illuminating a few inches below so Kye could just see where Dani's tail began and the sliver of skin between her scales and her vest.

Dani rested her good arm along the decking and took a long swallow of the whiskey.

"Thanks," she said, coughing a little as it went down.

Kye took a drink next and twisted the lid back on, setting it within reach.

"You really should go in and get some rest," Dani said, laying her chin on her arms.

"I might as well just sleep out here, keep an eye on you two."

"That makes almost no sense," Dani said. Her eyelids were heavy after the drink. "And besides, it's chilly. I can tell."

"You can keep me warm," Kye said, lifting back the sleeping bag opening and climbing in. They laid down and propped their head up close to Dani's.

"You know I can't keep you warm," Dani said in a husky whisper. "I'm cold-blooded."

"Well then," Kye said, leaning a fraction closer to her and whispering, "I'll just have to drink more whiskey. It's basically a sweater for your insides."

"You need to sleep," Dani whispered, pulling the sleeping bag up so only Kye's face poked out. Their long, sandy hair was a tangled mess, thrown up into a bun who knew how long ago. They'd clearly washed it and then wrapped it back up immediately without taking the time to comb through it.

"I don't think I can sleep," they said softly.

"Turn around," Dani said. "I'll comb your hair until you do."

Dani could hear her own heart pounding when they nodded, turning over so their back was to her. They shivered as Dani tenderly pulled their hair out of the tie and gently worked out the biggest tangles. Their skin felt warm under her slender fingers which were cool on their scalp, and she slowly worked out all the knots in Kye's long hair. Dividing it into sections, she combed through each, careful not to pull too hard.

They should both be sleeping, Dani thought. But the only sound was the gentle lap of water against the wood. Even the frogs on the shore had quieted down for the night. It was as though their pocket of the lake was an island away from all the dangers that lurked.

It was so quiet, Dani heard Kye's breath catch when she ran her fingers along their ear, moving the hair out of the way.

Her hand froze, resting against the space behind Kye's earlobe.

Slowly, tentative, she moved her fingers forward along Kye's jaw. Like it was something delicate and so very breakable. Dani's fingers reached Kye's chin, and she paused, holding her breath.

Then, with a slow exhale, she softly turned Kye's face toward her, sliding her hand to behind their other ear. Then she stilled again.

Neither of them moved.

Looking only in each other's eyes. Dani knew if she looked anywhere else something would change. She held Kye's gaze, not daring to breathe.

"I'm glad you're okay," Kye barely whispered.

"I don't think I'm okay," Dani breathed back.

"I'll do anything to keep you okay," Kye said. And their eyes flickered down, to Dani's mouth, for just a fraction of a second.

But it was enough.

Kye tilted their face up slightly, and Dani couldn't help herself. She moved her thumb feather light along their top lip, tracing their cupid's bow, then back to their jaw.

"You need sleep." Dani closed her eyes.

"So do you."

"I don't want to sleep," she breathed.

When she opened her eyes, Kye was staring at her.

Then Kye said, "Dani."

And Dani gave in. She pulled Kye's face to hers, their lips almost touching. Kye gasped. Dani's heart pounding so hard she thought it might be making its way out of her chest.

"Kye," Dani said, her breath tickling Kye's cheek.

"Yes?"

"May I kiss you?"

Kye inhaled sharply then let out a gravelly, "Yes."

They expected a crushing blow, but Dani moved as though any sudden motion would scare them away.

She traced Kye's lips with her own, her fingers trailing along their chin. The smallest flick of her tongue on the side of Kye's lip. Her mouth cool as lake water, both of them tasted like honey whiskey.

Dani let out the smallest whimper, and it was Kye's turn to make a sound she'd never heard from them. Reaching their hands up, they pulled Dani the last fraction of an inch closer until their lips met completely.

The fear of the other running from this fell away as their kiss deepened until Dani was breathing from her gills not lungs and Kye had to pull away to catch their breath.

Both of them were breathing hard, not looking away from the other.

Kye rushed in for another kiss, but Dani said, "Wait."

And the crushing disappointment that crossed Kye's face gave Dani the audacity to laugh. She gave Kye a quick kiss and held their face.

"We really do need to rest, and if we keep doing this right now, I'm going to keep you up all night on this dock," Dani said, smiling at Kye. "But we are going to get back to whatever this is, I promise you."

"Okay, I'll live with that," Kye said, reaching for the whiskey and taking another small drink before passing it to Dani.

"Now," she said, "lay down so I can fix all the mess I just made of your hair."

Kye leaned forward and kissed Dani tenderly. "Fine."

It didn't take nearly as long for Kye to fall asleep as they would have expected. But Dani stayed awake much longer, braiding their hair, and keeping watch, knowing that tomorrow, everything might be in ruins.

Chapter 25 Kye

Before the sun had even begun to rise, Kye woke up more rested than they had any right to be. Especially given everything they were about to attempt.

Dani had disappeared into the water at some point in the night, and Kye figured she should get as much sleep as possible so slipped up the pier quietly. They could come back and wake her and Billy with breakfast later if there was time. Dragging the bedroll behind them, Kye made their way up the walk to the house, where Florence, bless her gigantic perfect heart, had already put on a fresh pot of coffee and started a large pan of bacon.

She was not in the kitchen at the moment, but Kye assumed that she was brushing her teeth or something, and when she came back in a minute later, Kye gave her a big hug.

"Hey." Florence hugged them with a grin.

"Hey," Kye said back.

She poured them both mugs of the hot coffee, adding some cream to Kye's. She set them on the island and took a seat on the kitchen side so she could fuss with the bacon and whatever else she decided to cook up.

"Did you get any sleep at all?" She raised an eyebrow at Kye.

"More than I might have." Kye sat down, cupped the coffee mug in both hands and sighed contentedly as they took a big sniff. It smelled amazing. Florence must have brought it in from their favorite coffee shop in the city. "Mmm. Thank you." They took a small sip to keep from burning their tongue and savored the nutty flavors. "Best part of waking up."

"Sure thing." Florence took a sip herself, and Kye could almost see her relishing the warmth and instant hit of caffeine. "Your hair looks beautiful, by the way."

"Huh?" Kye reached their hand up to their hair and felt rows of braids and twists. "I'll be right back, gonna brush my teeth."

"I'll be here," she said in a way that made heat rise to Kye's cheeks.

In the bathroom, Kye shut the door behind them and leaned into it, closing their eyes for a moment before turning to look in the mirror.

Dani had outdone herself. Kye's hair was done in a large braid down the center of their head, but on one side, Dani had woven in shells and what looked like twists of copper wire so their hair was looped through them all the way down the side. It was delicate and fierce, and she'd obviously done the most intricate work on the side that was showing while Kye slept better than they had in their entire life.

Where she'd found the ornaments, Kye had no idea, and how she'd done it while Kye had slept really freaking soundly for being on the dock, Kye couldn't figure out either.

But to be honest, they weren't thinking about it too hard.

Just about Dani's lips on theirs and her fingers running across their neck.

Kye was gonna need a lot more coffee if they were going to get their brain on track. There would be no focusing on the doom situation without the help of caffeine.

Lots and lots of caffeine.

They brushed their teeth and quickly washed their face. Then went back to the kitchen. The smell of bacon was blessedly strong as Kye entered the room.

"So, how was your night?" Florence asked when they came in.

"How was yours?" Kye shot back, eyebrow raised as they took the seat across from her.

"Mostly I listened to my Calm sleep aide app for what felt like three hours before I gave up and watched reruns of Bewitched. So, I'm completely sleep deprived, and my therapist is gonna have words with me," Florence said with a shrug. "How about you though? You slept on the dock?"

"Yeah, you know, fresh air and all that." Kye took another drink of their coffee and started peeling an orange from the bowl on the table.

"Fresh air?" Florence gestured at Kye's hair then crossed her arms, eyebrow raised in a knowing best friend for life sort of way.

"And, like, Dani and I kinda kissed."

"What!" Florence squealed, flinging her arms out and knocking her entire coffee mug off the island, spilling it everywhere. She didn't even pause to worry about it but actually jumped up and down twice and clapped like a thirteen-year-old at a Claire's for the first time.

"Oh my god, Florence, calm down." Kye laughed and grabbed a towel from under the sink to mop up the spilled coffee.

"I will absolutely not calm down Kye James Miller. I swear to sweet baby Jesus that if you don't tell me every single detail in the next thirty seconds, I will murder you and throw you in the lake then spend the next twenty years of my life playing victim and no one will catch me."

"Dang, Florence, that is really grim." Kye knew that outlandish threats of violence were her way of expressing love, so they just shook their head and laughed.

"Tell. Me. Everything."

"I don't really know what it means, and we didn't, like, talk too much." Kye wasn't sure what to say about it, and if it was anyone but Florence, they'd have kept all thoughts to themself. "I sorta fell asleep right after."

She nodded. "Well, I want details when you're ready, but in the meantime, I have to ask. Do you want to kiss her again?"

Kye grinned and nodded. Which sent Florence into another fit of squeals.

"I am so so so so so so so so so happy for you." Florence wrapped Kye in a gigantic hug.

"Okay, okay, let's eat breakfast before you lose your voice from all this squealing."

Florence busied herself with bacon and toast and passed a jar of peach jam to Kye, who slathered it on their piece.

"So, I've been thinking about Tara." She took a bite of bacon and a sip of coffee.

"Yeah?" Kye prompted, reaching for another piece of toast.

"Do you think they went back for her?" she wondered, a sad look on her face.

"I don't know. They seem so single-minded. Maybe not."

"We could go back and check on her," Florence suggested.

Kye shook their head. "We don't have time, and we gave her the opportunity to go with us and she refused."

"Yeah, but she's in a cult. It's not really her fault." Florence was upset, and Kye mostly just wanted to eat more bacon and get this day over with. Finding a way to get Tara out of a cult seemed like a lot of task to add.

"Maybe once all this blows over, but for now, we have to focus on the bigger picture. Call Sable if you want to have her check, but make sure she's careful." Kye stood. "I'm going to get dressed."

"It's probably a good thing you're the one with the powers." Florence picked at her plate.

"What do you mean?" Kye sat back down.

"You're just so brave," she pointed out. "I'm all worried about little baby cultists."

"First of all, an actual little baby cultist is my worst nightmare. Secondly, I'm not brave. I'm just doing risky things, and it's working out." There hadn't been much time for Kye to really think through what happened when their hands started glowing. It just seemed like an extension of themself.

But bravery hadn't crossed their mind. They were just angry that their friends were in danger and generally annoyed at Muir and the cultists.

"Well, either way, I feel bad that I'm glad it's not me." Florence frowned. "I don't think I could be making the same decisions you are."

"I can't really tell if you're wanting reassurance or what right now." Kye didn't know what she was getting at. They hadn't done anything special, so why was Florence pointing these things out?

"I'm not wanting reassurance." She looked confused. "I'm worried you're being single-minded in a way that is new for you. I want to make sure you're the one making the decisions."

"I don't know what that means." Kye was frustrated suddenly and did not understand why.

"Never mind." Florence poured another cup of coffee. "Just remember that sometimes focus needs to be more than on just one thing."

"Bigger picture and all that. Got it." Kye downed the glass of orange juice that Florence had summoned from the fridge. "Let's take some of this down to the dock."

Chapter 26 Kye

Fifteen minutes later, stuffed with bacon and toast and two more cups of guzzled coffee, Kye and Florence were arguing about the next step of the plan.

Dani and Billy looked on, munching on the food Florence had brought to them.

"This is an incredibly bad idea." Florence crossed her arms and scowled at Kye, who was pinning their hair up into a *Little House on the Prairie* bonnet, which looked ridiculous, and smoothing out their denim skirt, which was also ridiculous.

"I know that, but it makes sense." Kye tucked the long-sleeved button-up blouse into the ankle-length skirt they were wearing, that Florence had pulled from somewhere in the house. They smoothed out their hair and pinned on a brooch for good measure. "If there's a chance we can get in and stop the cultists before we have to fight them, we need to at least try."

Dani kept her mouth pursed, but Kye could tell she was really worried and probably thought the idea was as bad as Florence did. Why she was holding her opinion back, Kye couldn't quite figure out.

The plan made sense though, and Kye was determined to try and reason with Muir one more time. Plus, if there any chance of stopping the cultists before they got their plans underway, maybe they would be able to rescue Muir and keep the dam from getting damaged or destroyed or whatever else it was that the cult was planning.

"Look, I'm just going to one church service. It's not like I haven't been to one before. You just drop me off and then come back to get the harpoon gun mounted to the boat." Kye looked in the mirror Florence held and shuddered a bit but then reminded themself that this was just a costume.

They could totally pass as a prospective cult member.

"It still doesn't seem totally necessary," Dani said. "We already have the harpoon gun."

"Yeah and only two harpoons. I did good with the knives, but I had spares. I'd rather we do everything we can before we start shooting," Kye added. Dani nodded. "There might even be clues on how to beat whatever they're summoning."

"I guess it's not like they're gonna turn you away." Florence handed Kye a small stack of the brochures that were always being passed out that they'd collected from Muir's things. "They definitely seem keen on finding new recruits."

"True," Kye said, tucking them into the big pocket of their cardigan.

Other than Tara and Muir, hopefully none of the cultists would recognize them in their disguise.

"I wish I'd grabbed a few more knives," Kye said.

"What happened to trying everything before we start shooting?" Dani crossed her arms.

"Stabbing is so totally different than shooting." Kye bent down and tied their sneakers. "You can reuse knives."

"That is not reassuring." Florence gave a quick wave to Dani. They needed to get to the church for their sunrise service so Kye could hopefully sneak in as a new convert.

Kye turned to head up the dock but paused when they felt Dani's hand on their ankle. Looking down, Kye couldn't help but smile. "I'll be careful, promise."

Dani nodded, giving their ankle a gentle squeeze that sent a shiver up their spine.

They got into Florence's truck, and she dropped Kye off well out of sight of the church building.

"This is such a shit idea," Florence muttered.

"It's just church." Kye rolled their eyes. "Come back in an hour. I'll wait for you here."

Florence shook her head and didn't move the truck until Kye was out of sight around the corner. Kye knew because, despite their bravado, they were reassured by their friend's lingering presence.

Jes McCutchen

Kye made their way down the path to the church, which was lined with a wide variety of angel statues that looked like they'd come directly from a garden center megastore. Their reasonable shoes carried them to the entrance through the small parking lot. They had been to enough new churches in their life to have some pretty solid assumptions about how the service was going to go.

To absolutely no one's surprise, those assumptions were quickly stamped out.

And Kye wondered, for not the last time that morning, if they should have listened to Dani and Florence.

An older lady at the entrance held the door and greeted them with a huge smile, a pamphlet, and blank name tag for Kye to put their name on, which was par for the Oklahoma church course. The greeter asked many questions, but it all seemed pretty normal for a small church in Oklahoma. Especially after Kye showed them the pamphlets they'd brought as an explanation for what had brought them there.

"This is such an exciting time for you to be here," the lady grinned widely, not showing her teeth. "You'll be so glad you made this decision."

Kye wasn't totally sure that their decision was quite what the lady was referring to, but they definitely didn't seem like they were going to kick Kye out.

However grateful Kye was to be tucked to an elder in the church like a little chicken, the woman led them to a seat very near the front, and Kye's little Presbyterian heart balked at sitting quite so close to the altar, even if it was a super small building to begin with. But they were there to gather any information they could, so they accepted the gentle pat of the woman's gloved hand on theirs and sat in the narrow pew, taking a seat on the purple cushion.

Everything seemed about right for the first five minutes or so.

Until the service started.

They weren't even pretending to be a good old-fashioned country church anymore. About twelve seconds into the start of the service, announced by the familiar chimes of an organ playing, everyone in the congregation pulled on dark blue cloaks from huge baskets that cultists were walking down the aisle. Each robe was embroidered in silver on the back with the same patterns that were on all of the cult stuff. Kye was never going to be able to get that pattern out of their head.

Kye sort of sheepishly giggled and leaned toward the old lady at their elbow, asking, "Do you have an extra one for a visitor to borrow?"

The lady just turned and shook her head. "You won't need one, dear."

Cool, Kye thought to themself. Cool cool cool. Not ominous at all.

"What the Hades are you doing here?" a voice hissed from behind.

So much for no one recognizing them. "Good morning, Tara. You sleep okay?"

Kye turned and looked at Tara, who had obviously not slept okay and was still in the same dirty basement clothes as the night before, just covered with a fresh cloak. Florence would be relieved to know she'd made it out in once piece.

"You really shouldn't be here." Tara huffed under her breath, tugging on her robe.

"What's wrong, Tara, miss your morning coffee?"

Tara looked at their bonnet, "You look so freaking absurd."

The old lady gave both Tara and Kye a look, and Tara narrowed her eyes at her.

"Mind your business, Ms. Nadine." She said it in a tone that made Kye grimace and worry Tara was about to get slapped, but the old lady just looked aghast and pulled on Kye's arm so that their attention was directed toward the front.

The lights dimmed, illuminating the stained glass. The sun was rising and its light filtered through the stained-glass windows.

Which, Kye noticed suddenly, were all very much water themed and also resembled imagery of merfolk. It was simultaneously jarring and unsurprising.

Then, as if well rehearsed, the dozen or so church members stood abruptly and moved to the edge of the room where each spread a container of what looked like salt along the walls. The grandma stayed with Kye, who could think nothing except what in the Will Rogers fuck was going on.

Then the chanting began, and Kye was glad their hair was in the bonnet because a wind picked up from inside the church.

On the stage was a small pool, which Kye had assumed was used for baptisms. And maybe it was, but that was not their plan today because Muir suddenly surfaced from inside the water.

"How in the world?" Kye muttered under their breath, though it earned them a sharp look from Ms. Nadine.

Then, to Kye's surprise, the lady whispered an answer, "It's connected to the greater lake through a tunnel. And our world is too small to contain the multitudes."

"Oh, cool?" Kye didn't really know how to respond, but it did explain how Muir had been able to attend services.

Nadine added. "We raised the money for it through a bake sale."

"Oh, okay." Kye again wasn't sure what to say. "Good for y'all, I guess?"

Speaking of Muir, it wasn't just a place for him to enter. He was basically on display.

As the sound of the chanting grew, Kye looked around, trying to find anything that might help disrupt what they were doing. They had a dreaded feeling in the pit of their stomach that any extra time they had to explore other avenues to stop this mess had evaporated. If anything, Kye was thinking they'd just wasted a few precious minutes on excursion.

Searching through the small sanctuary for anything that might help, Kye had a growing sense of doom about everything that was happening.

This was bad.

Not to mention, they were annoyed at the totally non-traditional service structure and the total lack of even a sermon to maybe point them toward some sort of clue.

Behind Muir, a wall of water rose up the back of the church.

Kye gaped.

This had gone from PBS nature documentary to Cthulhu really freaking fast.

With a burst, the water surged, and the wooden wall blew out, revealing the lake, which was no longer the calm and peaceful home they'd always loved but a burbling and churning deep blue cauldron.

Muir raised his arms and rose with the wall of water, which pulled him backward onto the lake.

All around Kye, the members of the church were chanting in what was possibly Latin but definitely not a language they'd ever heard spoken aloud.

It didn't take a genius to realize they were calling forth the octopus or cephalopod or whatever that creature they'd seen in the photos at Mr. H.'s was, and it was definitely happening right now.

Kye wanted to just nope out of there, but the creepy old lady kept tightening her grip every time they tried to pull away from her. Ms. Nadine's nails clutched Kye's forearm through her gloves, and there would be bruises if not worse. Kye was really hoping she didn't break the skin.

Then the old lady turned and looked at them, and Kye decided fingernail cuts were probably going to be the least of their worries.

The woman's eyes had gone solid neon yellow, never a good sign.

And her teeth were elongating into sharp points like a gar. It grinned back at Kye with unblinking eyes that had an uncanny resemblance to the alligators they'd fought in the bog.

Turning back to look at Tara, Kye saw her shake her head and then stretch and crack her neck.

"You really shouldn't have come here," she said.

"Tara? What's happening?" Kye could see her injured hand, and even the broken fingers were elongating like Ms. Nadine's teeth.

"The Rising." Tara's voice was warbled and scratchy, her jaw stretching in a yawn that seemed to never stop. "The Flood."

Right, so this was definitely turning into an "abort the mission" type of situation, but they hadn't really thought that far ahead. And even if Kye had been able to get to their phone, there was little chance they'd have reception, and they were still many minutes away from the one-hour pickup time they'd planned with Florence.

Plus, there was another giant wall of water beginning to form around the cultists right outside their circle of salt.

Kye just had to hope that everyone noticed the giant freaking change in the lake and came to help.

Chapter 27 Dani

Dani, Florence, and Billy were working to get the harpoon gun attached to the front of the fishing boat when they had, in fact, noticed the giant freaking change in the lake.

Dani was not handling it calmly.

"We are going to go get them out, now." Dani gritted her teeth together and pointed at Florence's truck. "I'm coming with you."

Florence protested, but Dani gave her a look and said firmly, "Either I'm hopping in the bed of that truck, or I'm driving it, tail or no. Imagine what I'd do to your clutch."

That got Florence's attention.

Billy started to say he was coming too, but Dani cut him off.

"You stay here and keep working on the harpoon rig," she said. "We need it ready, like yesterday. We'll be back as soon as we can. You can set up the welder for when I get back."

"Dani, here." Billy handed her the dagger she'd let him hold onto, and she tucked it into her vest along with its twin.

"I'm not liking all this stabby stuff," Dani grumbled but double checked that both weapons were secure.

The lake was turning into a complete mess, and Kye was right in the middle of the most dangerous part. Dani had just let them waltz into that building, all of them knowing full well it was full of baddies.

Florence nodded and raced to the place where her truck was parked just off the deck. Dani hurriedly made her way across the dock, scooching and, not for the last time, lamenting the prominent use of wood in human lake houses. At least Kye's family kept theirs maintained.

"Come on then, Bruno." Dani climbed into the bed of the truck, waiting impatiently to close the bed until Bruno had hopped in. He seemed more awake than usual but not by much. She gave him a scratch on the head, and he rewarded her with a lick.

Bruno might not make a good guard dog, but he was a great therapy dog. As if hearing her thoughts, he gave her another lick and plopped his head on her lap.

Florence floored it around the lake to the spot where she had dropped Kye off. "We never should have let them go."

"Yeah, I really don't think either of us was gonna stop this particular steamroller of an idea." Dani spoke through the open cab, watching as they approached.

Whatever magic these folks were spewing, worked fast, and Dani was kicking herself for letting Kye attempt to infiltrate this madness, even if she and Florence wanted to find a way to help Tara if they could.

When they got to the spot where the church had stood less than an hour before, she had to make herself breathe.

Florence slammed on the brakes. "Holy mackerel."

From what they could see, the church was still there and intact but surrounded by blue-and-green water that spun around it in giant swaths, obscuring the view of the church and roaring like a tornado. There was algae and driftwood and freaking fish spinning in the wall of water.

It was moving quickly, but Dani could make out chunks of rock and logs and whole ass turtles in the mayhem. It was like the bottom of the lake was being dragged up and made into a whirlpool barrier. Presumably to keep anyone else from interfering.

And it would have worked.

Except for two things.

One, Dani was pretty sure she was totally in love with Kye.

And two, Florence was one of the fiercest best friends on the entire planet.

"We have to go get them," Dani shouted through the open window into the cab.

Florence gripped the steering wheel and tightened her seat-belt.

"Duck," Florence yelled back and put the truck into gear.

Then she floored it and drove the truck straight into the swirling wall. Picked up by the pull of the water, the truck swung around the edge of the small sanctuary then came to a stop inside near the front where Muir had been minutes before.

Miraculously, the truck didn't hit anyone, even though they were all lined up in a circle with their creepy robes and candles that stayed lit in the wind. Dani looked around frantically, wondering where the heck Kye was.

The truck had taken out a section of pews.

"Florence," Kye called from across the circle. "Dani?"

"Jump in," Dani shouted.

But Kye was unable to wrench free of the cultist who gripped their arm.

Dani watched as Kye elbowed a really old granny right in the freaking nose, blood spurting from the wrinkled face. Even at that distance, she and

Florence could see that there was something twisted and shark-like in the cultists' faces.

Their mouths and jaws were too large, and their eyes glowed an eerie shade of yellow.

Creepy faces aside, seeing Kye break that granny's nose might have been the most unsettling thing Dani had ever witnessed them do, but they were able to break free of the granny's grip, but they didn't run directly to the truck. Instead, Kye turned toward one of the cloaked figures.

Dani recognized Tara quickly and watched as Kye shook her by the shoulders and pointed to the truck.

The old lady was recovering, and several of the cultists seemed to be breaking out of their chant and turning their attention to Kye. As their chanting continued, albeit haltingly, the walls of water seemed to weaken and cave in slightly. Dani had a horrible vision of the water giving way and collapsing on all of them, turtles and barrels and dead fish and all.

If it all fell at once, the weight might crush even the truck.

They needed a distraction if they were all going to get the heck out of there before the cultists lost all focus or finished whatever it was they were casting.

221

"Hey, you turds, wouldn't you rather have another merfolk to do your magics with?" Dani shouted over the din, waving her tail over the bed of the truck so it was visible in the eerie light.

That definitely caught their attention.

Apparently, this whole merfolk power business was a legit draw for cultists. They turned almost as one and took a step toward the truck.

"Kye, get in here," Florence hollered over the noise, honking her horn.

Finally, whatever Kye was saying to Tara seemed to get through, and the two of them pushed past the group of cultists and leaped into the back of the truck.

"What the living heck did you do to your truck?" Kye gaped at the debris-covered mess.

Florence ignored them and put the truck into gear.

Which was when Muir made an appearance.

Rising from the lake through the whirlpool, the tumultuous riptide parted as he moved through it. Dani could see him over the tailgate, and he was almost unrecognizable.

His tall, tan body and short, blond hair blew in the gale. The tattoos glowed a deep purple. And he was massive. Twice as big as he was before. His insides seemed to bulge against his skin and scales.

Like they might all just pop out if someone poked him with a big stick.

"Friends!" His voice boomed, amplified by magic, and every word rang out and echoed in the cab of the truck and across the lake. He moved forward, his body propped up by the column of swirling water. "Get back here. You belong with me."

Least friendly vibes ever, Dani thought.

"Hold on tight," Florence shouted over the boom in Muir's voice and floored it.

Gripping Kye's arm with one hand, Dani gave Muir a little wave then ducked low, pulling Kye down with her as the truck barreled back through the water vortex for a second time. They came out on the edge of the parking lot, and Florence was able to get the truck back on the road quickly.

The drive back was even faster than the drive there, and Dani was impressed at how focused Florence was. She thought that she should probably offer to chip in on gas once this was all over.

"What are we going to do with her?" Dani nodded toward Tara.

Tara was curled up on the floor of the truck bed. As soon as she'd gotten in, she'd collapsed and lost consciousness. Her cloak covered her body, but through it, they could both see she was shaking.

"I couldn't leave her this time." Kye put a hand on Tara's shoulder.

She shrugged it away, the cloak moving enough to reveal that she, too, bore the long rows of teeth and her hands were stretching into claws, though they were not as large as those of the other cultists.

"That looks really painful." Dani furrowed her brow and moved over closer to Tara.

"Based on how happy they were when it happened, I don't think they're feeling pain right now." Kye knelt next to Dani, holding onto the side as Florence hurried home. Dani noticed they kept looking behind the truck on the road, but it remained empty.

"Just because they don't show it doesn't mean they don't feel it. There is some major darkness in this magic." Dani needed to help Tara. She felt it in her gut that she could.

She looked over at Kye, who was pulling off their hat and wiping fish guts out of their clothes, the adrenaline of the last few minutes pumping through their entire body. Dani could practically see their energy vibrating.

Before she over thought it, she reached over and pulled Kye into a hard-and-fast kiss.

Cupping Kye's jaw in her hand and pulling them close with the other, she said, "That was a really foolish thing for you to do. You're not allowed to go on dangerous missions anymore."

A Mean Piece of Water

"You're the one who rode in a truck through a wall of lake." Kye looked her in the eyes, and Dani ached to have Florence drive them far, far away. Instead of continuing, Kye rushed in and kissed her again. For a second, the whole mess of things melted away.

Then the truck pulled to a scattered gravel stop.

Kye pulled away, determination set in their eyes. "We won't let them win."

Dani took a deep breath and nodded.

Chapter 28 Dani

Dani had been so distracted by the kiss it took her a moment to realize Florence had stopped in the middle of the road. They were idling just before the barrier that would take them into the safe zone surrounding Kye's lake house.

"Why did you stop?" Kye asked through the window.

"Because of Tara." Fortunately, Florence, who was grinning at them with waggly eyes, had realized before Dani or Kye, who were maybe sorta distracted by the making out, that they couldn't just drive through the protective wards with a member of the Church of the Flood, unless they just really didn't understand magic systems.

"Oh silt." Kye stood, suddenly alert, and watched the road. "I didn't even think about that."

"We can't exactly leave her here," Florence pointed out. "Any other ideas?"

Dani had been thinking about the wards, and though neither of them had had a chance to ask Mr. Harold about his magic, Sarnas had told her that there were wards of many types. Dani was guessing that Mr. Harold had put this one up.

"Kye, I think you can get her through," she said.

"How?" Kye narrowed their eyes and looked at the barrier. They hopped out of the truck, followed by Bruno, who just lumbered his way through, apparently not wanting to wait around for them to figure it out.

Dani and Florence watched as Kye put their hand against the air and the barrier let out a small ripple of red light stretching in all directions. The same color as the snake-like energy Mr. Harold had summoned back at his house.

"I don't want to take it down completely because this thing is freaking handy," Kye thought out loud. "But I think I can make a hole for a second."

"I like that idea more than driving through and possibly hurting Tara or just leaving her here." Florence had gotten out and was standing near the truck but kept a wary distance from Tara's claws.

The way the girl shook told Dani that she was fighting something. Tara may have walked to the truck on her own, but she was definitely going to need help getting out of it. Whether what she was fighting was internal or external or a combination of both, Dani could not yet tell. But she wanted to help Tara and was glad that Kye had brought her with them.

It only took a few moments, and Kye, hands glowing slightly—it was almost too dim to see in the daylight—had widened an opening in the wards enough for Florence to drive the truck through. Florence wasted no time, and Kye stepped through and closed the opening behind them.

"How did you do that?" Florence put the truck into gear, and Kye hopped in the back.

"I'm not really sure." Kye shrugged. "I just wanted to protect Tara and get us through to safety."

They were almost to the house, and Dani watched Kye, who was still intently staring at the road behind them.

"What did you say to her?" she asked.

"Huh?" Kye turned to Dani.

"What did you say to make her come with you?" Dani knew it had been the right decision but wanted to figure out how, after all the refusal the night before, Kye had convinced her so quickly.

"I told her not to let all those group projects go to waste." Kye's eyes shone with a steeliness that Dani had become familiar with over the last forty-eight hours, and they shrugged. "And that I hoped she was a strong swimmer, just in case, but that we were gonna win."

Florence pulled the truck to a stop in the driveway, and she and Kye hopped out.

"Do you think you can get Tara to the dock for me?" Dani moved to the bed of the truck.

"Sure you don't just want us to tie her up again?" Kye came to stand at the end of the truck.

"Yes, I'm sure. I don't know if I can help her. But I'm going to try, and I think I need the water." Dani hopped down, her hips aching. She was so tired of being on land. Once this ordeal was over, she wasn't leaving the water for a month.

Kye whispered a few words to Tara and then scooped her up out of the bed of the truck and carried her down the ramp like she was a bag of feathers.

Dani took a deep breath and dove into the water next to Billy.

"How goes the harpoon attachment?" she asked.

"Y'all are gonna need to double check everything. But I think I got it in the right spot." Billy raised his shoulders in a shrug. "Eww. What is in your hair?"

He blanched as Dani raised her hand and pulled out a chunk of debris, not all of it plant matter.

"You don't want to know," she said.

Then he noticed Kye coming down the ramp with a bundle in their arms. "Who the heck is that?"

"It's Tara."

"From the basement?"

"No, another Tara from a cult. Yes, Billy, from the basement."

Kye gently lay Tara down on the dock and took a step back.

"What's happened to her?" Billy swam closer and peered at her distorted face. "She didn't look like that last night."

"Cult stuff?" Florence offered less than helpfully with a grimace.

Dani ignored them and dove under the water. She wasn't completely sure what she was looking for but knew she'd find it close by. Closing her land eyes and opening her water ones, she reached down and separated several types of plants in her hands, cutting a few that felt familiar from her time with Sarnas.

Surfacing with a handful of plants and algae, she shooed the others away and carefully pulled the robe back from Tara's form. She was still wearing the same worn clothes as she had been the night before.

Up close, she looked even younger than Dani would have guessed.

Tara convulsed and shivered, but her teeth and claws had not grown any more, and when Dani pulled her eyelids back, her pupils flashed between black and the glowing yellow that the rest of the cult had shown.

Kye knelt beside Tara. "It's not on you to cure her."

"I know that, but I at least need to make sure she doesn't go total cult monster and attack us while we sleep." Dani gently ran her hand along Tara's, the claws squeezing her fingers but not making a mark or causing any pain.

Taking a breath and letting her instincts guide her, Dani formed the plants and mud she'd gathered into a paste, spreading it across Tara's forehead and belly. Then Dani closed her eyes and, concentrating, placed one hand over the poultice and thought healing thoughts.

Her hands began to glow, and Tara instantly stopped convulsing.

A few moments later, Tara had drifted into a restful sleep, her body still and her breathing steady. Though her face and hands remained long toothed and clawed, the lines in her forehead relaxed, and there was no more evidence of further teeth or claw growth.

"Do you think she'll wake up?" Kye asked after a few moments.

Dani pulled back and rinsed her hands in the lake water, leaving the mixture on Tara but pulling her shirt back down and smoothing her hair out of her eyes.

"Eventually," Dani said, "but not for a while. We should move her inside, where she'll be more comfortable."

231

Kye nodded and reached down to scoop Tara up.

When they did, Dani noticed their arm was bleeding.

"Come back, and I'll take care of your arm before I finish mounting the harpoon gun." Dani couldn't help but notice how effortlessly Kye carried the sleeping Tara as they made their way up the steps.

While they were gone, Dani swam a few circles, stretching away the calm sleepiness that had seeped into her while she was healing Tara.

Kye came back quickly. "I put her in the guestroom, and Florence is making sure she's comfortable. But whatever you did, she's dead to the world. Do you think her teeth and hands will ever not be so pointy?"

Dani shrugged. "I have no idea. I just wanted to make sure she was out of pain for now. Her insides were fighting her brain." She let out a shiver. "Let me see your arm."

"I'm fine. You might want to save your energy for welding on the harpoon rig." Kye pulled their sleeve down over the marks.

She sighed at them. "Sit down, Kye. I'm gonna fix it. You can rest for two seconds."

In a clear act of masking their nervous energy, Kye popped off their shoes and sat down on the dock with their feet in the water. When Kye was worried, shoes off, toes in the lake was the first step in getting them back on even footing.

"Let me see it." Dani reached her hand out and gently took Kye's arm, pulling it close and carefully lifting up the sleeve Kye had covered it with. Kye had changed out of the rest of the clothes from their quick cosplay as a conservative church-goer.

"It's fine." But Kye winced when Dani touched the spot where moon-shaped fingernail claw marks had scratched the soft skin on their forearm.

Dani felt before seeing that infection was starting already. "Well, I'm guessing cultists don't take too much care to wash under their demon-summoning claws, so let's let me take a stab at healing it before we have to chop your arm off because it's gangrenous."

Kye pulled their arm back. "You wouldn't."

Dani laughed softly at their over-the-top dramatics. Kye smiled slightly and gave their arm back to Dani, who used some more of the poultice and gently rubbed it into the bloody wounds on Kye's arm.

"I guess if it becomes possessed, then you could chop it off."

The area warmed up under Dani's fingers, and Kye let out a small content sound.

Dani almost lost all of her concentration.

She gently massaged the area until the wound had soaked up all of the salve and then permitted herself to continue the careful touch for a few minutes longer than necessary. Kye's eyes were closed, and they looked relaxed for the first time since they'd fallen asleep the night before.

It wasn't until she heard Billy clear his throat and Florence walking down the ramp that she stopped.

Dani hadn't worn herself out. If anything, she felt energized and like she could heal an entire army. Letting go of Kye's arm, she ran her hand down their calf, giving it a gentle squeeze under the water.

When she looked up, Kye was looking at her with an intensity that was welcome.

Dani saw behind it that, if she could heal an army, Kye could handle one.

Chapter 29 Kye

"So, can you do that healing thing to my truck?" Florence walked up as Dani was finishing healing Kye's arm. They felt like they could run a marathon. Whatever healing magics Dani was gaining were working wonders.

"For you, Florence, my dear, I would try." Dani laughed and swam to the boat, lifting herself into it. "But really, how are you doing?"

Florence shrugged and shook her bottle of emergency meds. "So far so good."

"Y'all got everything you need?" Kye stood and watched as Billy assisted and Dani got to work with their makeshift harpoon rig.

"Your folks are gonna be so mad when they see what we're doing to their boat." Billy looked away as Dani flipped down the welding helmet and quickly tacked on the base of the harpoon.

"I'm just glad I got my dad that portable welder for his birthday," Kye said. "It's come in really handy."

"Bet he didn't realize we'd be using it for something like this." Billy patted the harpoon gun gently as Dani worked.

"Yeah, it was pretty much just for fences and stuff." Kye nodded toward the metal fence they'd helped him put in around the patio.

Dani flipped up the helmet and glared at them. "Can you two stop chattering and let me focus for one second?"

"Right, sorry." Kye held up their hands and mimed zipping their mouth shut. Dani looked so cute in the helmet, with the scowl of concentration on her face. Much more like the project-loving Dani that Kye had always known.

"How'd she learn to do this anyway?" Billy asked quietly, and Kye had him hold one end of some rope so they could untangle it while Dani worked.

"We aren't always chasing after cults, you know," Kye said. "Dani is capable of a lot more than any of us give her credit for."

They were impressed at how much Billy had stepped up in the last twenty-four hours. He'd always been the tag-along younger distant cousin pain in the butt. But Kye was glad he was there right then.

"Okay," Dani said, nodding to Kye to switch off the rig. "That's as good as it's gonna get unless you want to take a whole lot more time."

She gave the harpoon gun a shove and smiled with satisfaction when it didn't topple off the boat. They all assumed Mr. Harold would rather they tack it on and possibly tarnish some of the original metal than for it to, like, accidentally dump into the lake.

"I'm going to get the harpoons." Kye turned to walk up the ramp back to the house.

"Kye, wait one sec." Dani pulled off the helmet, tossing it onto the deck and diving into the water. When she emerged, she was holding Emmylou Harris out to Kye. "She'll hate it, but can you toss her in like the bathroom tub with some food?"

"Of course." Kye gently took Emmylou and set the giant frog on their shoulder. "I'll leave a note for my folks, just in case something happens."

It seemed right. They weren't really in the mood to explain everything that was happening and was about to happen in a note or anything like that. Their parents were out of town. Way, way out of town. And who knew what they were going to come home to.

But Kye could write a note explaining that Emmylou Harris was a beloved pet and how to take care of her. So Kye did just that, scratching Bruno behind the ears. "I suppose you're not gonna let me lock you in the bathroom with a bag of dog food until this is all over, are you?"

Bruno just gave them a withering look and turned to have his neck scratched at a more efficient angle.

Adding a fairly lengthy portion to the note about how they should be super careful opening the guest bedroom and that there might be a werewolf-looking shark teen locked in there, Kye went ahead and also jotted down the Sparknotes version of The Church of the Flood.

The last thing they added was a line about how much they loved them.

Then they stuffed it in an envelope, and using all caps and a red marker, they wrote "OPEN ASAP" on the outside and taped it to the interior garage door that their folks always used when they'd been driving.

Emmylou safely deposited, Kye hurried to their room, grabbed the harpoons, and threw on a windbreaker, opting for shoes that favored traction over waterproofness. They popped Bruno's doggie life vest on, much to his chagrin, and on the way out, grabbed a few beers. Because even if it was only eleven thirty in the morning during the apocalypse, it was five o'clock somewhere.

Kye slid the deck door closed and hollered to Florence, "You about ready? We're fixing to go."

She nodded and gave her truck a pat, whispering something Kye couldn't make out.

The two of them hurried down the dock, clipping on life vests and those water-activated emergency blinking lights as they went, Bruno loping behind them. Billy and Dani were double checking the gun mount for what Kye guessed was the seventh time when they got to the end of the dock with Florence.

Both of the merfolk hopped up onto the platform. Kye and Florence took seats, and Kye handed out the beers.

"Do we have time for this?" Florence sat crisscross and popped hers open.

"The Flood can wait." Dani opened hers as well and handed one to Billy.

"I get one?" he asked, surprised.

Florence rolled her eyes. "You can have like one sip for a toast."

Billy didn't even grumble and seemed content to be included at all. Hopefully after this, they could do some more bonding with him and let him know how much he'd been appreciated throughout the last few days.

"What are we toasting to?" Dani looked at Kye with a wink when she asked, and Kye felt a flush creep up their neck.

"To not getting sucked through the freaking dam?" Billy suggested.

"Or to not letting an evil cult flood the entire planet with gross pollution water?" Dani added.

"I mean, that kinda covers it all?" Florence shrugged and took a swig of her beer.

"Sure," Kye said with a small smile at Dani. "That pretty much covers it."

"To not getting sucked through the freaking dam." Dani raised her bottle, and they all clinked. After taking more than a small drink, Dani turned to Kye. "Could you double check all my straps?"

Kye was glad they'd taken a small sip because it sounded much more intimate than Dani had meant it. But they nodded, and Dani turned around, moving her long braids out of the way.

Her vest wrapped around her front and tied in the back. Kye carefully undid the loose knot then retied it, using a sailing knot, their fingers lingering on the small of Dani's back where her scales met her skin. Kye couldn't tell if Dani's breathing changed, but theirs did.

Florence cleared her throat.

"Right, looks good." Kye patted Dani on the shoulder, quite smoothly.

"We have to go." Dani took another drink then set her bottle on the deck and hopped into the water.

Kye and Florence both stood, and Billy hopped in the water as well.

"Go team?" Kye said.

"We already had our toast." Billy took his position next to the boat.

"Yeah, Kye, don't try to draw it out," Florence added, stepping into the boat.

"For real, let's not get overly sentimental." Dani surfaced and grinned at them.

"Y'all are mean," Kye said.

"Just hop in the boat, Kye. Let's go save the day." The worry behind Dani's eyes mirrored what Kye knew was in theirs. So, they nodded and stepped onto the boat, followed closely by Bruno.

All of them gazed out at the horizon, now purples and blacks and glowing blues.

It was no longer possible to ignore the silhouettes of tentacles rising from the water. Growing ever skyward. Clawing their way up to the surface.

Chapter 30 Dani & Kye

Dani

As soon as Dani swam past the barrier wards, the sound of the boat was drowned out by the churning lake.

"That's a mean piece of water," Kye yelled over the rumble of thunder in the clouds that hung so low they almost touched the surface.

Dani dove under and, using her senses other than sight, could tell that the lakebed, too, was rolling. There had been a huge earthquake at the lake a few years ago, and it felt similar to then, only it wasn't stopping after a few moments. The water table seemed to be fluctuating more and more as they swam closer to the center of the lake. She was grateful that, so far, the violent movement was centered in the lake, far from their underwater homes and not yet reaching all of the land dwellings. But the movement was getting larger, and the pulsing waves were getting stronger.

Swimming on the surface, they could see more and more distinctly the tentacles that rose out of the water. Emerging from the purple glow in the middle of the lake, the arms of the creature were long, and even from a great distance, Dani could make out suckers lining the appendages and spines on the outer edges.

"I can't see its head," Florence yelled over the rain.

"It might not have one," Kye responded, a shudder coming through in their voice.

"How close are we gonna try and get?" Billy asked from the other side of the boat.

This was nothing like the races they'd done last summer, speed boat versus merfolk. And Dani had the feeling in her gut that she should turn Billy around and send him straight to Sarnas, but it was too late for that.

"I have to be able to aim at something." Kye pushed the boat forward. "If we can't find its brain, maybe it has a heart?"

The silhouette of the creature was lit by lightning and a glow emanating from the vortex that held Muir aloft. Dani had always known Muir would do something ridiculous, but this was not what she'd imagined. His body seemed triple its normal size, having grown exponentially since they'd left the church less than an hour ago, and she worried he might explode.

Like, literally burst open. His wafer thin skin was barely holding his insides on the inside.

He was chanting and calling toward the creature, pulling power from the vortex created by the cultists that held him aloft and amplified his booming voice. They were not yet close enough to hear what he was saying, but the gist was: come and get it.

Diving under again, Dani was able to feel that the vortex of water he rode on stretched all the way from the cultists to him and then to the lakebed and was doing its fair share of tearing things up like a tornado across land. The massive size of both the monster and Muir made it seem like they should reach them any second, but they just kept getting bigger as the boat and the merfolk pushed forward.

Then, Kye cut the throttle on the boat so it was almost to a stop, bobbing in the swelling waters.

"Look," they shouted, pointing ahead.

"Not more gators. I hate these gators." Florence hadn't even faced them, but they were her worst nightmare. With good reason. Dani knew she'd be having bad dreams about them forever.

The eyes of at least two dozen of the milky white creatures peered menacingly at them through the whitecaps. Pulling up short, Dani spun around and realized that there were more to the back of them, swimming fast. She didn't know how they'd managed to cut them all off, but they had.

"Get in," Florence yelled, beckoning to Billy and Dani.

But Dani shook her head. "We'll sit too low in the water with the harpoon gun too. You two go. We'll get past them."

"No way," Kye yelled, reaching their hand out as if to pull Dani up.

Instead of taking their hand, Dani reached into her vest and handed Billy one of her two daggers.

"What are you doing?" Kye looked livid.

"We'll catch up," Dani said and pushed off from the boat. "Go."

For one long second, Kye held her gaze, and Dani thought they wouldn't push on. But then Kye gave her a quick nod and pushed the boat to full throttle as the gators closed in.

She turned to Billy with a nod.

"We got this, Dani." He turned so they were back to back, and the two of them ducked just under the surface of the water so nothing could sneak up on them from below.

Kye

Kye pushed the boat through the phalanx of alligators, and for a gut dropping second, they thought the boat would tip over when half a dozen of the powerful creatures thrashed against the side as they sped past, trying to knock the whole boat into the water. But both Florence and Kye thought fast and leaned against the tilt so they were able to

245

speed by. Kye had to grip the steering column with both hands to keep from looking back to check on Dani and Billy, but right now, they had to focus and get this nightmare over with.

There were so many tentacles Kye couldn't count them all.

"I thought octopuses had like eight arms," Florence despaired.

"That's not an octopus," Kye commented the obvious.

"Well, it has about eight trillion arms. And those arms definitely seem to have brains of their own, so I'm sticking with octopus."

Kye couldn't disagree and slowed down enough that they could switch places with Florence and prepare the harpoon gun, thankful that the two of them had spent so many hours over the years begging their parents to let them take turns steering the boat, pretending to be pirates or captains.

"How much closer?" Florence struggled to steer against the choppy water but pushed onward.

"I have to get close enough to aim this thing. And I'd rather not miss," Kye shouted from the bow.

It was hard to tell what the best thing to aim for would be, and the water was getting even rougher. They barely had any experience with waves since the lake was always calm and when it stormed, they stayed inside. But Florence was doing a really great job of steering, and in minutes they were within twenty-five yards of the creature.

The urge to look away from the other-worldly demon was almost insurmountable.

But Kye forced themself to look at it. When they did, they could see that it definitely had a head. Its many glowing eyes blinked rapidly, and the swirling water around it rocked and swayed the tiny boat.

"We need to try to get a little closer." Kye had the harpoon gun loaded and was prepared to take a shot, but the flailing tentacles made it hard to know if they'd be able to hit it.

"I'll try," Florence shouted back, trying to steer the boat nearer the demon.

Bracing their knees on the gun, Kye pressed their hands around the trigger and focused, willing the harpoon to light up like it had in the forest.

But nothing happened.

They thought really hard about how great it would be to demolish this gargantuan demon octopus.

No glow.

They tried to focus on how extremely ticked off they were at this whole situation.

Still nothing.

"Oh silt." Kye groaned.

Chapter 31 Dani & Kye

Dani

There were so many more alligators than there had been in the river. It was a frenzy in the rough waters. Looking around at the approaching monsters, Dani and Billy dove straight down to see if they could get past the horde, but the gators followed them.

"We should split up," Billy called, but Dani disagreed.

"We can outrun them," she shouted back, and they sped off together as quickly as they could.

But the tumult under the water was slowing them down.

Plus, having to dodge debris and swim in the mud was harder for them than the gators, which seemed to just bulldoze straight through the flotsam. Everything was chaotic, but they were staying close together, until suddenly, they weren't.

Dani wasn't sure what had hit him, but just as she thought they might get past the blockade and outrun the creatures, he swam full speed, straight into something as solid as a seawall. She noticed immediately and spun to grab him as the first gator that caught up clamped its giant maw around his fin and the water filled with black blood as it bit down through his scales.

Billy screamed.

Dani wrenched the dagger from her vest, stabbing the alligator in the eye. Blood spurted out, turning the muddy water even darker as the blood from the gator mixed with Billy's.

But the stab in the eye worked, and the massive animal released its strong jaw from Billy's body and roared angrily. Then, buying Dani a few seconds, the next three alligators turned like magnets to the wounded one, and Dani didn't stay to watch as they ripped its body apart.

In the frantic few moments that passed, Billy had fallen unconscious and there was still a horde following close behind. Dani was obviously slowed down significantly, having to drag him with her.

There were so many of them. Maybe if she was able to stab a few more, they could just eat each other. Though the likelihood of her getting a perfect eye shot five more times was slim, and by the time they got close enough to stab, they'd be munching on one of them, which wasn't better.

But she was determined to protect Billy.

She had to think. And fast.

But it was too much too fast.

How would she get them out of this?

Protect Billy.

It might have been the panic, but suddenly, Dani felt a clarity, and wrapping her arm around Billy like a lifeguard, she sensed a bloom of the algae Sarnas had used in her healing close by. She jerked them both toward it, and the spot lit up in a phosphorescent glow. She spun them in a tight circle, clutching Billy, the glow lighting up the algae in the water and turning it to a teal bubble surrounding them.

After she spun twice, the sound of the choppy water completely stopped, and all she could hear was Billy's heart and own her rapid breathing. Through the green mist-like water surrounding them, she could see the alligators abruptly stop their hunt.

They looked confused and disoriented. As though suddenly forgetting what they were chasing.

She tried to hold her breath, not at all sure whether they could hear her. But after a few moments, they turned around and, scattering, swam quickly in as many different direction as there were animals.

"What the heck?" she whispered.

And she realized that she felt stronger and more focused than she had in days.

Letting instinct drive her actions, she reached down to Billy's open wound and ran her hand along the puncture holes and tears that the jagged teeth had made. She felt the scales repairing as simply as if she had zipped them back together. There were not even a marks where the alligator had clamped down.

He remained unconscious, but Dani knew he was going to be safe where he was in the still-glowing bloom.

Giving him a quick kiss on the forehead, she swam out of the bubble, leaving him nested in the green water, and raced back to the direction she'd left Kye.

Kye

So, being angry definitely wasn't going to work. Kye tried to get their hands to go glowy over and over, each time yelling out in frustration.

"We're running out of time." They slammed their hand against the harpoon gun.

Kye barely registered it when the creature's tentacles lashed out, narrowly missing the side of the boat. More and more of it kept emerging from the portal, which swirled a sickening yellow and purple.

"You're already out of time." Muir's voice boomed over the din of the storm and the wailing screams emanating from the creature.

"And you're still a dick," Florence shouted at him.

It made Kye smile for half a second. Then they realized what he meant.

The creature was moving. No longer climbing up from the hole in the lake, it was pushing itself toward the dam. Its gargantuan body pulled their boat and all manner of debris in its wake.

"It's moving toward the dam," Kye shouted, pointing south. "We have to cut it off!"

Florence nodded and gritted her teeth, pushing down on the gas and steering the boat around the creature. The only luck they had was that the gargantuan size of the demon slowed it down, as it stretched itself from the portal center.

Kye held onto the bow and the harpoons as Florence steered their vessel around trees and dead fish. In moments, they were between the creature and the dam.

Kye cried out in frustration again as nothing they did activated the harpoon weapon.

Then, from out of nowhere, Dani popped up right alongside their boat.

"Kye," she yelled, and Kye whipped their head in her direction. "You have to think about protecting us. Not about destroying it. Protect us."

It was like a light switch.

Kye went from being angry at Muir, angry at the monster, angry at that ridiculous freaking cult to determined that their friends were getting out of this.

Florence would be safe.

Billy would be safe.

And Dani. Dani would be safe.

"Turn us around," Kye yelled to Florence, who spun the boat in a U-turn twenty yards from the approaching monster.

The simple change in focus did what Dani must have known it would, and the harpoon lit up in a red glow as soon as Kye placed their hands on the weapon.

Aiming directly at the creature's many eyes, Kye took in a breath then let it out and fired.

It missed.

All it did was strike a tentacle and really piss the demon off.

"Oh crap." It was all Kye could do to not to just nervous laugh until the creature swallowed them all up. And if had just been Kye, that might have been how it went down.

"Stop thinking so hard." Dani swam alongside the boat.

"Hey, creepy lake thing, look over here," Kye shouted and started waving manically.

"I don't know if that's what I meant!" Dani grimaced and braced herself as the creature swung one tentacle then another.

Kye did not know what they were doing, but it was their turn to let instinct steer the ship. They grabbed the unloaded harpoon and lit it up.

They held it over their head and shook it at the creature. "You ready for another go?"

"What are you doing?" Florence yelled.

Kye refused to look back at their friend.

"Kye, wait," Dani said, and if they weren't certain they were about to do something exceedingly foolish, Kye might have pointed out that Dani was being rather contradictory.

"Come and get me," Kye whispered, wrapping themself around the harpoon as another tentacle swept across the deck, dragging them into the stormy waters with it.

Chapter 32 Dani & Kye

When Dani saw Kye wrenched off the boat by the monster, she didn't hesitate and, aside from sparing a brief backward glance at Florence and Bruno to assure herself that the boat remained afloat, dove in after them.

Kye's breath was knocked away by the tentacle strike, and they were being pulled into the center of the beast. Eyes closed in the murky darkness of the muddy waters, Kye was battered against piles of debris and dead fish and the crushing grip of the spikey tentacle suckers.

But they knew every scrape was going to mean the beast's downfall.

Every one of the thousand tiny cuts.

They clutched the harpoon gun, its warmth increasing in the frigid waters.

Dani swam swiftly. Her focus was only on reaching Kye. She let the instinct to heal guide her, and through the tangle of tentacles and lake debris, she worked her way closer, like finding the center in a maze. Her gills flexed, and through the water, she could sense Kye's pain and injuries.

She swam faster.

Kye was determined. This thing wasn't supposed to be here. In their lake. Attacking their friends. Hurting their neighbors.

Threatening to flood the entire freaking earth.

Even as they felt the blood draining from their body, they used that softening to harden their resolve. Pouring all their force into the weapon. Until it wasn't just a harpoon anymore but an extension of their will.

And their will was an unwavering and un-distractible singular focus.

As was Dani's.

The beast pulled Kye in. If it had had a mouth, it would have swallowed them. But the maw they entered was indescribable. Not that they ever planned on describing it to anyone.

And Kye knew it was time.

Reaching inward, the harpoon clutched in their arms—now red hot as lava—pulsed once then twice, and then, with the power of what felt like a nuclear bomb, it exploded.

The same moment that Kye set off the explosion, Dani, at full speed, grabbed them, separating Kye from the harpoon, and in a barrel roll, they were both enveloped in rushing green and tossed around like those ladies who used to send themselves off of Niagara falls in barrels. But less fancy and a thousand times more terrifying.

Dani cradled Kye in her arms, her tail wrapped defensively around them both, holding Kye's head and neck as steady as she could.

Without thinking, she was taking an inventory of Kye's wounds, and without undoing the protective barrier she'd created for them both, was healing what injuries she could as they spun closer toward the collapsing portal.

Kye awoke with a start.

They shook from the grip they were in for a moment before opening their eyes and realizing it was Dani who held them. Kye's lungs were tight, and they tried to pull in a gasp of air, expecting to suck in water.

But instead, there was nothing.

They felt like they were going to black out and began to panic.

Then Dani pulled Kye in for what they thought at first was a well-timed apocalypse-is-imminent kiss, but their lungs filled with something akin to oxygen.

Dani looked into their eyes and mouthed, Don't panic.

Kye nodded.

"Get ready," Dani said as whatever they were surrounded by crashed onto the lakebed just as the portal collapsed in on itself.

Dani swam to the surface as quickly as she could, pulling Kye with her. The protective bubble kept them shielded from the tousled debris. Once they broke through the surface, Dani was relieved when Kye coughed up a lung full of water, and blurted out, "Monster fuck."

The demon was gone, and Kye was breathing.

That should have been the end. But when Dani looked up, holding Kye tightly to her chest, the vortex Muir controlled was still strong.

And he glared at them both from the top of it.

His body twisted in rage. The tornado of water holding him aloft pulsed and swelled until he was almost on them.

Kye wiped the hair out of their eyes and scowled. If they could take out that demon octopus, they could handle this douchebag.

Dani felt the change in Kye as they took a deep breath. She still clutched to them, keeping them both afloat, and when Kye began to heat up, Dani could feel it.

The energy surrounding them both was gaining.

They had to stay together, and Dani stretched her arms along Kye's, as they reached theirs forward. Kye didn't need a knife or a harpoon or luck this time. The energy was in them, and the shield they felt from Dani behind them filled Kye with confidence and resolve.

With a scream that pulled straight from the inside of their body, Kye pushed all the energy they had at the vortex Muir was controlling.

Dani felt the pull of the water and the thrust of Kye's power as she pushed her energy into Kye, urging them on as they tore at the magic that held Muir aloft and also keeping them from pushing too far.

Tempering Kye's power. Knowing it was natural and focused but, without control, could hurt them.

Kye was happy to pull that audacious dick off his cult-made pedestal and did so.

With a final yank, they focused their energy on the center of the vortex and severed it in half. The slice of their arms sent Muir crashing into the lake water yards away.

Dani grabbed a piece of floating debris and hooked Kye's exhausted body onto it, making sure their life jacket was still clipped on, and swam the short distance to Muir, who had landed unconscious in the water. Using the same technique she'd used on Billy, she surrounded him in a binding water cocoon.

Kye clutched the board that Dani had put them on and coughed up what felt like their remaining lung.

Not literally. That would have sucked.

Dani used her powers to pull Muir toward them, onto the surface of the water. He was limp but bulging, and she had wrapped him in a swirl of green.

And then, just as Florence pulled the boat up alongside them, Kye blacked out.

Chapter 33 Dani

With Florence's help, Dani pushed Kye into the boat. They were dead weight but breathing. Dani wasn't sure if it was her healing that had knocked Kye out or the immense use of power. Mr. Harold had collapsed similarly after casting his spell, but Sable hadn't seemed extremely worried about his recovery, which gave Dani hope that Kye would wake up soon.

With a grunt, Florence pulled Kye onto the floor of the boat.

The water was still rough, and there was endless flotsam that had been dragged up from the bottom of the lake and now floated at the top. Once Kye was secure, Dani had to figure out what to do with Muir and pulled him closer to the boat.

"Toss me some rope." She caught the rope Florence threw her and wrapped it around Muir so they could pull him with the boat.

It was then that the sound of helicopters could be heard in the distance.

The sky was clearing, and the sun was beginning to peek through. Apparently, someone from either the National Weather Service or a local news station had finally decided to pay attention to the giant storm that had flared up over the lake.

"We gotta get going," Florence called to Dani. "I don't think any of us wants to have to talk to whoever is flying that thing."

Dani agreed. "You take Kye and Muir. I have to go get Billy. I'll be right behind you."

Florence nodded. "Is Billy okay?"

"Yeah, he's going to be fine. I'll see you in a minute," Dani reassured her before diving under.

The lake was messier than it had ever been, and all the torn-up debris was making it hard to breathe. There was so much pollution in the garbage that had been churned up. It was going to wreak havoc on the creatures who called the lake home if they'd survived the attack.

As she swam to where Billy rested, Dani realized she could sense the problems in the water, like she'd sensed the wounds on Billy and Kye. Not slowing down because getting Billy out of the tumult was her focus and she didn't want to leave Florence alone with three unconscious people for long, Dani reached out her thoughts.

Experimenting.

She trailed her hands wide through the water and could feel the oils and gasoline that remained. Imagining her hands were magnets, Dani pulled the pollution to her, balling it up into something contained and manageable. It was going to take practice, but she was going to be able to heal the lake, just like she'd healed her friends.

With renewed energy, she sped forward.

The trail she left behind her was clean, healthy, fresh water.

When she got to Billy, he was still sleeping restfully. She shook him awake carefully.

"Billy, hey."

He looked at her and groaned. "Did I get eaten?"

She laughed. "No but almost. I think you're gonna survive though."

"Did I dream an alligator tried to take off my tail?"

"Nope, that definitely happened. But I healed you."

Billy looked down at his tail, the scales were unmarred. "Where are my scars?"

Dani smiled. "There are none. I'm getting really good at this healing thing."

"Well, that sucks," he grumbled and crossed his arms.

"What are you talking about?" Dani huffed. The Billy she knew was shining through like the last two days of responsibility and teamwork hadn't happened.

"Battle scars, Dani. Geeze. No one is gonna believe me about any of this." Then he had the audacity to roll his eyes at her. "I wanted to show them off."

"Right, so never healing you again." She gave him a big hug that he first seemed surprised by but then melted into. "Come on, kid. We gotta go check on all our friends."

When they got to the dock, Florence had already parked the boat and managed to pull Kye onto the decking. She had Billy help her cover the boat with the tarp so it didn't look like it had been out on the water lately.

"Are you okay?" Florence knelt down so she could look him over.

Billy lifted his tail into the air. "I got eaten by an alligator."

Florence looked confused. "Well, you look like you're in good shape."

"See what I mean?" He yanked his tail back underwater and glared at Dani.

"Don't even ask." Dani continued untying Muir and pulled him under the pier. She wasn't sure what to do with him, but he wasn't going anywhere for now. Hopefully, Sarnas would be able to help her figure it out.

There were at least five helicopters circling the lake, particularly near the dam and the Church of the Flood.

So far, they hadn't spent much time circling near Kye's lake house, but the merfolk had to stay hidden. Plus, there was the matter of the very human-turned-monster cultist currently resting in the guestroom that no one wanted to explain to the authorities. Dani guessed it was only a matter of time before people started knocking on every lake house door, but for now, Florence said the police scanner was just a total cluster of mayhem with no one knowing what in the heck had happened.

"I'm going to get the wagon and take Kye up to the house if you think that's best." Florence finished tying down the boat tarp.

"Yes, get them inside before someone spots you with a body." Dani was tempted to follow them, but between Billy, Muir, and the risk of being spotted, she needed to stay under the water.

Florence got the wagon, lifting Kye into it carefully.

"I think you're getting stronger." Dani smiled as Florence flexed her muscles.

"The better to drag my friends around this dang lake." Florence heaved and pushed Kye up to the house.

"Let's not try to make a habit out of this," Dani called after her.

While Florence was gone putting Kye into a bed, Dani used rope and straps that Florence had dragged over from the deck for her to make a kind of hammock under one side to secure Muir into.

He was awake and seemed quite angry but was slowly shrinking, which Dani took to be a good sign. The fresh tattoos that covered his body seemed to be fading. Not to the point where they were gone, but as though they were many years old. Her encasement seemed to be holding as well, but she still wanted to keep a close watch on him.

"Need anything else from me right now?" Billy asked after they had Muir's cocoon resting securely.

Dani shook her head. "You go rest now. I'll wake you up if anything earth shattering is about to happen."

Then to Dani's surprise, he swept her up in a hug. "I love you. Don't tell anyone."

She laughed and hugged him back. "I love you, too."

While she waited for Florence, Dani spent some time experimenting with her water-cleaning powers, assuming they would come in handy and give her and Billy a clean place to sleep.

Florence returned with two beers and a large sun hat and sat on the dock, handing the hat to Dani.

"Isn't it a little early for a drink?" Dani laughed and popped on the hat. If a helicopter passed by, they'd just see two people sharing a beer on a dock, watching the goings on so they could gossip with their neighbors later.

"On apocalypse day, it's always five o'clock." Florence clinked her bottle against Dani's.

"Amen to that." Dani took a long drink and looked out at the lake. The barrier that had separated Kye's lake house area from the rest of the lake had dissipated. The two of them watched as the layer of debris on the surface of the lake made its way toward them as it spread out.

"Are y'all even going to be able to live in that?" Florence gestured toward the water.

"I don't know." Dani frowned. "Not right away, but I think me and Sarnas will be able to help it."

"I'm glad the school is with her and safe," Florence said.

"Me too. I hope we're able to get in touch with her soon." Dani was worried about her hold on Muir, as well as the waters and the school.

"I was able to get a hold of Sable." Florence gestured to the landline phone she'd brought out to the dock with her. "She said Mr. Harold is awake and they're going to come as soon as they could."

"You're amazing." Dani reached up and gave Florence a hug.

"Okay, okay. Sure." Florence looked at Dani with eyebrows raised. "So, what's this about you and Kye making out?"

Chapter 34 Kye

Kye woke up and squinted against the sunlight streaming in through the window. They were in their room, and someone had covered them up in a quilt, probably Florence.

Bruno rested at the foot of their bed and opened an eye when Kye sat up.

They didn't have on shoes but were wearing soggy clothes. With a groan, they rolled over and looked at the clock, which read 4:42 pm. Kye felt like they'd been asleep for twenty-four hours and had a frantic moment when they thought that maybe they had been, but a secondary glance at their clock reassured them that it was still Wednesday.

With a huge stretch, they swung their legs off the bed and stood, looking for their shoes which someone, probably Florence, had taken off.

Kye honestly didn't care what all was going on for the moment and went to the bathroom across the hall from their room, where they stripped down and took the hottest shower they'd ever taken in their life. They didn't even feel sore in a painful way. Just sore in the way they felt after going on a long bike ride or spending a day swimming. And upon examination, their body didn't seem to be injured at all.

When they closed their eyes and tried to imagine the monster they'd fought, there was almost no clear image they could conjure up. As they dried off, they tried to draw it in the steam on the bathroom mirror, but everything they sketched was just a blob.

Kye went back to their room and pulled on a pair of sweatpants and a hoodie. Their hair was still in the braids Dani had done, but the mess they'd been in was unraveling things fast, so they spent a few minutes pulling their hair into a ponytail. Grabbing their sheets from their bed and bundling them with their wet clothes and towel, Kye stopped by the laundry room and started a heavy-duty cycle with the contents of their arms.

Bruno followed them into the kitchen, where Kye opened the pantry and scooped a large spoonful of dog food out of the container and dumped it into Bruno's bowl.

Bruno laid down on the tile and seemed to pout at the dry meal.

"You've been spending too much time with Florence." Kye scratched his head and, opening the fridge, pulled out the carton of vegetable broth that Florence always brought with her to add to his food.

Once they poured a splash onto the dry food, he was more than happy to gobble it up. While Bruno

269

ate, Kye assembled a plate of ham-and-cheese sandwiches, a bag of baby carrots, and a jug of iced tea. When they were done and Bruno had finished his meal, Kye walked down the hall to the guestroom and opened the door.

"Hey, Tara." Kye entered the room, closing the door behind them.

Bruno followed and plopped himself directly in front of the door.

Kye walked over to Tara, who was sitting up in the bed, wrapped in the comforter like it was a shroud.

"Hi," she mumbled, pulling the comforter over her more tightly.

"So, I'm pretty sure we won." Kye took one of the sandwiches and pushed the rest of the plate over to Tara, who hesitated then reached a clawed hand out and grabbed the bag of carrots, pulling them back behind the covers.

Though they couldn't see her face, Kye could hear the crunch of the carrots as Tara nibbled on them tentatively at first then with more gusto.

"Are you a vegetarian?" Kye asked tilting their head a bit as they ate their sandwich.

Through the covers, Tara shook her head, so Kye pushed the plate closer, thinking Tara might decide she wanted to eat the sandwich after all.

After a few moments, she mumbled through her jagged teeth, "If you won, it means my folks lost."

Kye didn't respond for a moment. "Yeah, I suppose that's true. It also means that a whole lot of people aren't dead."

For a minute, she didn't do anything, but then she reached her hand out and took the sandwich that Kye had offered her.

The two of them munched silently for a few minutes.

"What are you gonna do with me?" she asked softly.

"I'm not sure, Tara," Kye admitted. "But you should know that there are some really amazing folks who think you're worth keeping safe, and I pretty much do whatever they say most of the time. So, we'll figure it out."

Tara nodded. "Thanks."

"No problem." Kye took the last bite of their sandwich and stood, taking the empty plate with them. "I'm going to go talk to my friends. Do I have your word that you'll stay put? It's a much for your safety as ours."

"Yeah. I've got nowhere to go, so..." She trailed off.

"I'll be back soon to bring you more food if you want it."

"Thanks, yeah. That'd be great."

Jes McCutchen

As Kye made their way to the door, Tara called out, "Hey, Kye, two things."

"Oh yeah, what's that?" Kye turned, eyebrows raised.

"Um, does this TV work?" She pointed toward the small television resting on a dresser.

Kye opened a drawer and tossed her the remote. "And the second?"

"Is it okay if Bruno stays with me?"

"Well, that's up to him," Kye said, knowing full well that Bruno was going to stick around.

Scooping Emmylou Harris out of the bathtub on the way and taking down the note they'd left for their folks, Kye made their way down to the dock, where Florence and Dani were chatting. Both of them stopped talking when Kye walked up, and Florence bounced to her feet and wrapped them in a giant hug.

"You're awake." Florence looked them up and down. "Shouldn't you be resting?"

Kye set Emmylou down gently, and the frog croaked happily and jumped onto the pink donut inner tube Dani was floating in. "I honestly feel great."

"Glad to hear it." Dani smiled up at them.

"So, what are we doing?" Kye looked around the lake.

"Spotting helicopters and staying out of sight while we wait for Sarnas and Mr. H." Dani gestured to the circling emergency vehicles and pointed out one that was part of the National Guard.

"So far we've seen five news stations, the National Guard, and some all-black helicopter with no names on it at all." Florence sat back down and handed Kye a drink from the cooler.

"There have also been some sea planes from locals, but they've been getting hollered at by the cops." Dani gestured to the lake house to the north of Kye's. "They were not happy."

Word had gotten around quickly, and every local with a dock or a deck was sitting outside in lawn chairs watching the goings on, so Dani had to stay low in the water. But seeing someone in a sun hat, resting on an inner tube, was nothing out of the ordinary even if it was chilly.

If the authorities hadn't made it very clear that no one was supposed to be out on the water in boats, the lake would have been as crowded as the Fourth of July.

"Hey, check this out." Dani took one of the clear, empty beer bottles and ducked under the surface. When she popped back up in the tube, the bottle was full of gross, oily water. Holding both hands cupped around the glass, she concentrated, and the water cleared almost instantly.

"Whoa, that's amazing." Kye was impressed.

"Yeah, once all these yahoos clear out, I'm gonna try and get started on cleaning up the lake." Dani looked out at the polluted water with a sigh.

"I'll find a way to help you with that." Kye loved her ambition and focus. It wouldn't surprise them if she had the entire lake cleaned in a week.

Under the water, Dani rested her hand on Kye's ankle and gave it a gentle squeeze.

"For now, we're pretty sure we can just hang out though." Florence leaned back in the lawn chair she'd brought down and used the binoculars she'd taken from the house to watch the mayhem.

"What even is downtime?" Kye laughed.

Chapter 35 Kye & Dani

Kye

Early the next morning, the skies were still full of helicopters and small planes, and the lake was covered in official-looking boats as the folks in charge tried to figure out what in the heck had happened.

Dani was talking to Sarnas, and Kye and Florence spoke with Mr. Harold and his niece.

"Thanks for coming," Florence said to Sable. "It's nice to meet you."

"Why don't you two go on ahead and put on some coffee inside." Mr. Harold was clearly dismissing both Florence and Sable, but neither seemed to mind.

"Sure, Uncle." Sable walked with Florence to the house.

"We'll be back when it's brewed." Florence gave Kye a thumbs-up.

Kye admired just how quickly Florence seemed back to herself from three days ago and really hoped they'd get a chance to salvage the rest of their spring break plans with that movie marathon.

"I don't know what to do with Tara." Kye filled in Mr. Harold, and he nodded.

"She wouldn't be the first one that needed some rehabilitation. But it sounds like she got into it quite young. This is both a good and a bad thing." He poked at the chimenea, and Kye handed him some small sticks and paper, which the two of them began breaking up for kindling.

"How do you mean?" Kye helped him by tossing out the older pieces of charred wood.

"If she was young, that means it's easier for the people who are caring for her now to recognize that it wasn't her fault. Even though we know that cults affect folks of all ages and it's not their choice, it's gonna be easier for her to be accepted having been born into it."

"And the bad part?"

"Accepting the wrongness of something you've got ingrained in you is a mighty big hill to climb." Mr. Harold took the small pieces of wood that Kye handed him and arranged them over the kindling.

"What about the, you know, claws?" Kye handed him the barbecue lighter, and he started the small fire.

"Those will fade in time, but it will not happen right away. She'll have to earn that within herself. But she's not the first, and she won't be the last."

276

"And she can do that with Sarnas?" Kye wasn't sure how they felt about sending a girl they barely knew far south with someone they'd only just met, but it seemed like the best chance Tara had at coming out of this mess both unattached to the cult and not in FBI custody like the rest of the cultists presumably were.

Based on a quick bike ride to the former location of the Church of the Flood, as far as Kye could tell, they'd either all fled or the FBI or some other government secret agency had scooped them up. There was no sign of any of the members, and the place was crawling with tall, lanky folks in black suits and aviator sunglasses. They looked like they were in Men In Black cosplay.

"Sarnas will take her, along with Muir. But I can't say that it will be Sarnas who will do most of the helping. Sarnas belongs here." He gestured around the lake, which still had choppier waves than usual. The debris coating the surface looked like the trash compactor in A New Hope, and the sound of helicopters and sirens continued as they had for hours.

"Has someone from the Church of the Flood been helped before?" Kye couldn't imagine someone fully coming back from that sort of experience. And Kye had a passing worry that maybe they and their friends wouldn't fully come back either.

As though hearing their thoughts, Mr. Harold gave Kye's shoulder a pat. "Yes, and you and Dani will be fine as well."

"What about Florence?" Kye looked up at the house, where they could see her busying herself with the coffee and what looked like a giant plate of sandwiches. Kye laughed. "Never mind, she'll be okay."

"People, both humans and merfolk, are very resilient." Mr. Harold had the fire going, and the crackle seemed to cut through the chill Kye hadn't realized they'd been feeling.

"I still want to talk to her first. Give her a choice." Kye didn't think starting Tara off on her new life with a forced trip away with strangers was a great way to build trust.

"That's reasonable and also very kind of you. I'm sure Sarnas would agree." Mr. Harold gave Kye a pat on the shoulder.

"Looks like Florence is almost done with the coffee. I'll go talk to Tara now." Kye stood and walked to the house, grabbing two mugs and a couple sandwiches as they made their way to the guest room. "I'll be right out, y'all can take the sandwiches to Mr. H."

Florence gave Kye finger guns. "See you in a minute."

Kye knocked softly on the door and opened it when they heard a quiet, "Come in."

Bruno was sleeping on the bed with Tara, his head resting on her lap.

Traitor, Kye thought with a laugh.

They took the plate of sandwiches and set them on the nightstand. Tara muted the TV and sat up.

"So," Kye started, "we have a proposal."

Tara listened quietly, munching on the sandwiches while Kye laid out the plan.

Dani

After reassuring Dani and Billy that the school was totally safe and content upriver, Sarnas was reinforcing the binding Dani had contained Muir in. He was conscious and really mad, but most of the swelling in his gross, pumped-up body had gone back to his regular size. It was painful to watch his skeleton and tail shrink but also much less upsetting than his steroided-out massiveness.

Though based on just how many rude gestures he was throwing at them, Dani didn't feel too bad for him.

"You did very well, Dani." Sarnas finished what she was doing.

Muir hung in the water, able to move only so much. They could see him shouting, but no sound came through. Sarnas was impressed by the hammock Dani had rigged up as well.

Billy was recovering quickly and napped with his head on the dock, Emmylou tucked in his arms. Sarnas had double checked the healing that Dani had performed and murmured her approval.

"Have I always been able to do this?" Dani looked down at her hands and turned them over. They'd never been of much interest to her, and now they felt powerful and gentle and important.

"I'm not totally sure how it happens, but once it does, you can rest assured it was meant to." Sarnas reached her own hands out to envelop Dani's.

"What will I do with it?" Dani wondered, looking out at the lake. "I have some ideas."

"I'm sure you do." Sarnas smiled at her. "You'll do whatever is needed."

"How often do cults try to cover the entire earth in water?" Dani would much rather focus on cleaning the lake than fighting zealots.

"Not as often as you'd think." Sarnas paused. "But far more often than you'd like."

Dani and Sarnas swam to the portion of the deck where they could look up to the lake house from just under the surface. They could see Florence and Sable talking to Mr. Harold up on the deck.

It prompted Dani to ask, "What will we tell our parents?"

After thinking for a few moments, Sarnas replied, "That's up to you. Richard has kept his family close, but I preferred to keep mine at a distance. I never liked big crowds."

"That sounds like Kye." Dani watched as Kye walked back outside, and they caught each other's eyes. Kye gave her a small nod.

Sarnas placed a reassuring hand on Dani's arm. "You'll figure it out together."

"When will you be back?" Dani asked.

Sarnas had explained to Dani that she would take Muir south to a community of merfolk near the Antarctic, where he'd have the opportunity to atone for what he'd done. Hopefully, he'd be able to come back after some time, but Sarnas could not make any promises.

"I'll be gone for a few months to get both Muir and the girl, Tara, adjusted to their temporary homes."

"Is it a home or a prison or what?"

"That will be up to Muir and Tara. But you all have given them a chance at redemption."

Chapter 36 Kye

A few hours later, everyone except Florence, Kye, and Dani were on their way. Billy had insisted on returning with Sarnas to the school, where he would take charge of them again, staying upriver while Sarnas set off with Muir and Tara, and until Dani could safely secure enough clean water for them to return.

"I need to go over it with my folks," Kye said, "but I think I'm going to apply to help with the clean-up efforts."

Kye and Florence had been able to get onto some news websites, and the official scientific best guess was that there was a giant sinkhole and also a tornado and those combined caused the disruption on the lake. There was a call for volunteers to work with AmeriCorps to help with clean up, and it said priority would be given to locals with their own transportation who were eligible.

"How long will that take?" Florence frowned.

"It's a minimum one year. So, it kinda gets in the way of our fall plans." Kye didn't want to disappoint her. They'd been daydreaming of rooming together for a decade, and that had always been their plan.

"Sort of feels like it's something you're destined to do. The lake needs you." She wrapped Kye in a big hug. "And your parents will be happy that they won't need to find someone to dog sit when they're out of town."

It was so typical of Florence to only point out how things would help others, and Kye loved her for it. "Maybe you want to consider a gap year?" Kye suggested.

"I'll think about it, we all know the lake it good for my anxiety." Florence paused then added. "I mean minus the doom portions."

Kye laughed and gave her a hug.

"Plus, I suppose Dani is going to be sticking around as well?" Florence said with a wink and a nudge.

"Anyway, we still have three nights of spring break left," Kye pointed out. "Let's go see if we can salvage some of it."

The two of them walked back down to the dock, and Dani popped up to meet them.

"Want to come inside and watch some movies with us?" Kye realized that Dani had never actually seen the inside of their house and was suddenly concerned that they should go tidy up really quickly.

"We can set up the canoe in the downstairs." Florence had perked up at the idea immediately and went to get started without even waiting for Dani to respond.

"I hope you like popcorn because Florence makes some kick ass stove-top." Kye reached a hand out and helped Dani up onto the dock. They still felt stronger than they'd been before, but it didn't have the full-body vibrating feeling that had come with it during the past couple days.

Taking a look around to make sure there were no approaching helicopters or boats, the two of them made their way up to the deck and into the TV room, where Florence had already dragged the canoe and was filling it with water.

"You sure your folks aren't coming home early?" Dani pulled herself into the canoe with a small, purposeful splash.

Laughing, Kye took a towel from the clean pile of laundry on the couch and mopped up the puddle. "At this point, if they do, I'm not even going to worry about it."

"Oh yeah?" Dani grinned mischievously. "You're ready to introduce me to your parents?"

Kye knelt down and put their hands around her head and pulled her close for a kiss. It was soft and unrushed. There wasn't an impending apocalypse, and Kye relished taking their time.

After a few moments, they pulled away.

The sigh Dani let out sent a shiver up and down Kye's spine.

"First, I have to see how funny you think *Three Amigos* is." Kye kept a completely straight face.

"What?" Dani laughed.

"I mean it. If you don't think 'Stonehenge' is funny, it's over." Kye tried to keep from breaking into a smile, but it didn't work.

"Okay, so which are we watching first?" Florence asked. "*Sixteen Candles* or *Breakfast Club*?"

"Apparently there's been a change of plans and Kye is giving me a test of some sort." Dani took the overflowing bowl of popcorn from Florence, who raised an eyebrow.

"*Three Amigos*? My little buttercup?" Florence took a seat on the couch, pulling about four throw blankets over herself.

"Has the sweetest smile." Kye popped the DVD in and flipped off the overhead lights.

Dani shook her head and chuckled. "Y'all are going to quote aloud the whole time we're watching this movie, aren't you?"

"Obviously. It's part of the test." Kye took a seat on a couch cushion next to Dani and draped their arm across her shoulders. It felt really freaking nice.

Afterward

Tara had only been on the rocky island for a few days, but she was already settling into new routines. Sailing the sailboat was hard work, and at times, both Muir and Sarnas had to join her and Sable in the cabin when storms threatened to separate them. But it was work Tara enjoyed. It helped her to keep focused on physical activities, rather than think about her former "family" or the changes to her body.

Sarnas had assured her that her teeth and hands wouldn't grow any longer, which was a relief. But Tara was still not used to them. They made eating things like bread harder to manage, but luckily, most of her diet consisted of fresh fish that Sarnas—and then Muir—would catch for her and Sable.

The trip south had taken several weeks, and by the second, Sarnas let Muir out to swim without the shield to bind him. It hadn't been an issue to leave Tara out of any sort of bindings, since she had chosen to go willingly and they were in the center of the ocean for the majority of the trip.

Before they left, Kye had given her some clothes, including winter ones, for which she was grateful, as the weather had gotten colder and colder the further south they traveled.

Tara stood on the edge of a cliff, drinking a cup of tea through a metal straw, the mug warming her hands against the wind.

She'd spent most of the life she could remember on the edge of a lake, and the ocean was a vastly different thing to behold. She was pretty sure she'd never get over the view of the icy water churning and crashing into the steep cliffsides and jagged rocks jutting above the waves. The roar was constant as the days grew longer and longer.

There were fewer people, merfolk and humans, here than had lived at the lake by a large amount, but Tara enjoyed the sparseness. She hadn't like talking much before, and now that her jaw hurt when she spoke and she knew the first question anyone would ask her would perpetually be "Are you okay?" she was even less interested.

Which everyone here seemed content to give her space for, and she appreciated.

Even more so than the lake, people here seemed focused on taking their time with every task to do it properly. There was never a rush, and everyone had time to accomplish their chores.

Lately, Tara had taken to eating lunch with Muir by the small natural pool where he stayed. Every day, he first had to chip away any ice that had frozen and light fires that were positioned throughout the pool to keep it melted and warm enough for him to stay awake and not just slip into a winter's rest.

Sometimes, when she finished her own morning tasks, she would help him with the fires and finishing chopping chunks of ice nearest the edge

The pool was small, and the warmth from the fire reached the little bench where Tara preferred to sit.

They hadn't spoken about what had happened before they left, and Tara had no intention of being the first one to bring it up. But having someone she knew nearby while they munched on salted fish and freeze-dried sweet potatoes was a comfort.

"Sarnas and Sable leave tomorrow." Tara had heard Sable talking in the kitchens, letting the others know.

Muir nodded then looked away as he asked, "Sarnas came and told me last night. Are you going with them?"

When Kye had spoken to her, they'd promised her it was her decision. And that up until Sable and Sarnas headed back to Oklahoma, she was free to change her mind.

Tara shook her head. "There's nothing for me there."

"I thought the same thing." Muir closed his eyes and turned to look at the already setting sun. It would be winter here soon, and the hours of daylight would diminish to almost zero.

"At least the nothing here is a nothing I choose." Tara stood, taking their empty plates, and made her way to the kitchen.

Acknowledgements

Marem who read the first and absolutely garbage draft and whose feedback was invaluable. This book would be dramatically different without their notes. Thank you for eviscerating my initial draft like a demon alligator eviscerates its prey.

Marshall, thank you so much for supporting me in this endeavor. Gaius, thank you too, even if you don't realize you're doing it. I love you both so much.

Victoria for being so welcoming to me and my work. I'm so glad we've become friends. Support your local indie booksellers, folks. They are gems among us.

My B2 Weirdos who very much deserve to have shelves full of magical queer brown merfolk heroes.

Whitney and Jeni who have kept me from eight billion pitfalls that would have kept my writing from making it out into the world. And the indie author community. Never have I felt so much like people just get it.

Meredith - you already got the dedication, what more do you want me to say omg?!

My GoT twitch fam who keeps me focused and encouraged.

My crew at Arts@302. We're building something wonderful and it is so inspiring to do it alongside all of you.

Ezra & Maxi for giving my books such beautiful covers. You're both magical in your art and I couldn't ask for a better team.

And to my nieces, nephews, niblings, and cousins. I hope you know that you are all loved and valid and capable and clever.

About the Author

Jes lives in Tulsa, Oklahoma with her partner and their kiddo. As well as two weenie dogs, Rocket Xavier and Fable Rose Pond. Jes is a Science-Fiction & Fantasy YA author whose works are full of ensemble disaster queer casts and the occasional crime and/or alien. She loves board games, soft sci-fi shows, and using stickers in her planner.

"A Mean Piece of Water" is her second novel.

For updates about her current and upcoming words, visit: JesMccutchenWrites.com

www.ingramcontent.com/pod-product-compliance
Lightning Source LLC
Chambersburg PA
CBHW031337020726
47499CB00005B/1305